Comedy Dreams

SHUBHAM DAS

An Imprint of Maple Press Private Limited

Maple Press Private Limited
Sales Office A 63, Sector 58, Noida 201 301, U.P., India
phone +91 120 455 3581, 455 3583
email info@**maple**press.co.in
website www.**maple**press.co.in
Go to www.**maple**library.com for more e-books

Comedy Dreams *by* Shubham Das

ISBN: 978-93-88304-17-7

Printed at Repro Knowledgecast Limited, Thane

10 9 8 7 6 5 4 3 2 1

Cover Design @ Artyfino.com

Acknowledgements

The novel *Comedy Dreams* has been written under the constant guidance and support of my dear parents. This is to show my deep appreciation and sincere thanks to their endorsement and blessings. They have always provided me various platforms to express my views and ideas. They are my true mentors.

I am grateful to my teachers of The Air Force School, Subroto Park and Kirori Mal College, University of Delhi for their constant help and thought provoking discussions. Both the institutions have extended multiple opportunities to me to nourish my writing skills and imagination.

I am also thankful to my friends for their encouragement and motivation.

Last but not the least; I am highly grateful to the pblishing. com team for providing technical and mental support at every stage of this novel. They provided constant technical support in publishing this novel.

Prologue

It was a bright sunny morning in Versova, Mumbai. The streets were filled with people walking briskly towards their workplaces, children running to reach their schools on time. The dabbawalas running with loads of dabbas and giving loud instructions to each other to maintain their coordination. The housewives were heavily bargaining with the vegetables and fish sellers. I was travelling in a taxi, which had been stuck in a traffic jam since fifteen minutes. I was sitting with my wife, Madhuri Shukla, on the back seat. I was looking out of the taxi's window to have a glimpse of the Mumbai city, the city where I had spent the memorable years of my life.

Madhuri was sitting with our four-year-old son, Sagar, on her lap. Sagar was a very stubborn kid, who just did one thing-crying, crying and crying. Madhuri was trying different ways to pacify him, but his fuss was unstoppable. So gradually his continuous crying and the heavy traffic jam started irritating her.

"How much time will it take, bhaiya?" Madhuri vented her frustration over Sagar and the traffic on the poor taxi driver.

"Ma'am the traffic jams..."

"Couldn't you take a shortcut?"Madhuri interrupted the driver's statement.

"Ma'am, this is the shortest possible route. Since this is the office hour and almost all schools start at this time, there is traffic. But the traffic is temporary on this route. Once we cross the traffic signal, the road will be clear."

Sagar continued crying as Madhuri was chiding the driver. Madhuri was about to bust out at Sagar.

"Calm down Madhuri," I patted her shoulder and softly spoke to her. "At least we can taste the actual life of Mumbai in this way, apart from the tourist spots and the person whom we are going to meet..."

I took out my I-Pad from my carry bag, opened a Tom and Jerry video and handed it to Sagar. He stopped crying and watched the video. As he stopped crying, I saw Madhuri feeling relieved. But still I could realise the heavy deadlines of her travel agency, the load of our family on her shoulders and the stubbornness of Sagar had completely sucked out happiness and laughter from her life. Though she was sitting normally besides me, her eyebrows, lips and jaws had sunken down. It made me ponder that day-by-day, most of us are getting deprived of laughter and comedy and the heavy workloads are becoming silent-killers for us. However, various stand-up comedians across the globe, give us a medicine of laughter to reduce the effect of that silent killer.

By the way, I am Harish Shukla (Harry). I work as a Deputy Legal Advisor at a Bangalore-based company. I have come to Mumbai from Bangalore with my family to meet a very special person. This story is all about him. As the traffic started moving slowly, I continued to think about the requirement of comedy in our lives and that special person, with whom I have spent the memorable days of my life, THE DESI DUDE...

ONE

Ten years ago, New Delhi

I was in twelfth standard and I was an Arts student. Every Arts student requires very high scores to enter good universities. My Economics was a bit weak. So my dad searched for the best coaching centre for me named 'The Success House' in Pitampura for Economics coaching. It was near my house and was famous for its faculty.

It was my first class at the Success House. I departed from my home with a rucksack containing pens and a notebook. I never went to any tuition before. I entered the classroom and sat on the second-last desk, which was vacant. The other students were chatting among themselves about their schools, other coaching classes, etc. The classroom had a huge whiteboard and four air conditioners, which were necessary for a huge classroom with so many students.

In the meantime, another guy came and sat beside me. He was a thin boy with a small and spiny beard. He was brown complexioned. He was very skinny and bones were protruding from each part of his body. He wasn't carrying any notebook or bag.

After some time, our tutor, Raghav sir entered the room. He started the class with his introduction, which included his name, teaching experience, his style of teaching and then he moved to the Economics syllabus and the weightage of each chapter.

I was listening attentively, but my partner seemed to be lost in some other world. He was fidgeting with his mobile phone and was thinking about some other thing. After a few moments, he turned to me.

"What's your name, bhai?" he asked in a desi accent.

"I am Harish Shukla. What's your name?"

"I am Sameer Mishra. So you are also a UP wala."

Sameer looked very innocent, which was unusual from the wild and bold nature of the typical Delhiite boys.

"So, which school are you in?" he enquired.

"J. D. International School. And you?"

"I am in Kendriya Vidyalaya. It is close to J D International."

As we were talking to each other, Raghav sir spotted us.

"Hey you two boys, you are not supposed to talk when I am teaching. Do your talking outside the class, not here. Don't take this subject lightly." Sir looked angry.

The class got over and the students started leaving the room. As Sameer and I were sitting on the second last bench, we were among the last ones to leave the room. We moved out of the coaching centre and suddenly, Sameer stopped me.

"Harish, where do you stay?"

"Income Tax Colony, Pitampura. And you?"

"Hey, I also stay in the Income Tax Colony. What a coincidence!"

Both of us proceeded towards our colony. We were chatting while walking. As it was our first meet, both of us started interrogating each other.

"Which stream are you in- Commerce or Arts?"

"I have Arts," I said.

"I also have Arts. Wow. So how do you go to school?"

"My bus comes each morning to pick me from my residence. And how do you go?"

"My school van comes to pick me from my home. Harish, which place in Uttar Pradesh are you from?"

"My family is from Kanpur. But I am born and brought up in Delhi. My family is settled here. Which place are you from, Sameer?"

"I am from Balia district. My father got transferred to Delhi four years ago from Lucknow, when I was in ninth standard."

"Oh we are just interrogating each other," I said.

"Yeah, like a police inspector."

As we were talking and walking together, I could not imagine how the time passed so quickly. My home came. I said goodbye and entered my house. Sameer's house was two blocks away from my house.

As I got into the house, I saw my dad sitting on the sofa and reading that day's newspaper.

"Hari beta how was your first day at the coaching institute?"

"It was nice, dad. It had a large classroom. Raghav sir told us about the syllabus and the weightage of each chapter. Then he started the first chapter of Microeconomics."

"Nice. What else, beta?"

"I made a new friend named Sameer Mishra. He is from Balia district in Uttar Pradesh. He also stays in the Income Tax Colony."

"Balia. My aunt stays in Balia district. The place has historical significance. Balia was the first district of India to gain independence from the British colonial rule."

"Oh I see. First place to be free from British rule."

"The dinner is ready. Hari beta, please help me out in the kitchen," mom shouted from the kitchen.

"Yes mom," I replied and went to the kitchen to help her.

TWO

It was my second day at the Success House. I sat on the same seat. Sameer again sat beside me. I turned to him.

"My dad told me about Balia. It was the first district of our country to be independent of the British rule."

"Yeah. My grandpa also told me this. My earlier school was in Chauri- Chaura, which also has historical significance."

Today, two boys were sitting in front of us. They were listening to our conversation.

"So you two are also from UP," one of them said.

"Yes," I replied.

"We are also from UP."

"Oh nice," I said.

"What are your names?" Sameer asked them.

"I am Himanshu Trivedi." "I am Nitin Tripathi." They replied.

"I am Harish Shukla." "I am Sameer Mishra." We replied.

"Which stream are you pursuing?" I asked.

"Both of us are in Commerce stream."

In the meantime, Raghav sir entered the class. Raghav sir started his lecture.

"Good evening students. Today we will start the topic, 'central economic problems and their causes.'"

Himanshu and Nitin again turned to front. Raghav sir started making flowcharts on the whiteboard. I again found that Sameer was taking only few notes in his notebook. He wasn't making the diagrams. He was thinking about something else.

After the class got over, Himanshu, Nitin, Sameer and I moved out of the classroom together.

"Hey Harish and Sameer. Both of us have scooties. We will drop you at your homes," Himanshu said.

"No thanks. We will go on our own," Sameer replied.

"Bro, don't feel shy. Just sit behind us," Nitin said.

"Okay," I replied.

Sameer sat on Himanshu's scooty and I sat on Nitin's scooty. They drove it at high speed and dropped us at our homes.

Gradually, four of us turned into buddies. We were back-benchers at Raghav sir's classes. He often pointed us out for not paying attention in the class. After the classes, four of us used to go to eat momos at Ramu's Momo Corner. He prepared delicious fried momos. We also created a whatsapp group and named it FRIENDZ ZONE.

A month had passed like this. Raghav sir was annoyed and he shifted Himanshu and Nitin to the afternoon batch because four of us were creating a menace to his class. However, he retained me and Sameer in the same batch as other batches had no vacancy for additional students. One day, Sameer and

I were hanging out after the classes. He turned to me to say something.

"So what do you want to do after class twelfth?" He asked in a Desi tone.

"I have not yet decided. There are so many options available. What about you?"

"Well..." he stopped after uttering that word.

"C'mon Sam. Don't be shy. I will keep your secret."

Sameer gathered courage to speak up.

"Harry, frankly speaking, I am not much interested in studies. In fact I was never interested in studies," he had started calling me Harry.

So my guess was right.

"So, what will you do in your career?"

"I have one and only one interest bro, Comedy," Sameer said in a hush voice.

"What! Comedy!" I was shocked. I had heard for the first time that someone wanted to make his career in comedy!

"I love to crack jokes and funny 'shayaris'. I like to roast people. Whenever there is Teacher's Day, Children's Day and Farewell celebration in the school, students and even teachers insist me to crack jokes on the stage."

"Nice Sam. But how will you pursue your interest?" I enquired.

"I want to become a stand-up comedian. A Desi stand-up comedian," he took a deep breath and said this.

I was stunned. Stand-up comedian! Desi-stand up comedian!

Sameer took out his mobile phone and opened a video of the Teacher's Day of his school. In the video, he was wearing the school uniform and talking about different types of students in a very funny way. He spoke in a Desi accent. He also satirised the attitude of students during exams, deadlines of submitting assignments and their different ways of cheating.

The audience in the video as well as I started laughing heartily. He had a unique way of speaking.

"I think you should definitely follow your passion. Ha ha ha ha…"

"I also want to do that…"

"So currently, do you only perform in your school, Sameer?"

"Ya, most of my performances are in my school. But last year, I associated with a group based in Delhi that performs Street Plays, Drama, Music and Dance and Comedy at different places in Delhi. I have performed in the Farewell function of Manas Shiksha Niketan, Youth Day celebration at the Indian Habitat Centre, Anti- Smoking workshop at the Siri Fort Auditorium, etc."

"Wow."

"I have my own page named 'The Desi Dude' on YouTube, in which I upload my new vines and jokes."

"You never told me earlier about your talent. Today I will definitely watch your vines on YouTube."

"Yes sure," he was blushing while telling about his talent. I didn't know that a simple guy like Sameer had such a talent of making others laugh.

We reached my residence while we were chatting.

"Oh my residence. So Sam, I will watch your vines tonight. It was really nice to know about your passion."

"Please like, share, comment and subscribe my YouTube page," he grinned.

"Yes sure. Goodbye bro. Goodnight." We shook hands.

After dinner, I rushed to my room, turned on the mobile data and searched for the page 'The Desi Dude' on YouTube. I found various vines in which he had funny monologues. He mocked at the tantrums of Delhiite girlfriends, students before their exams, millions of students applying for UPSC exam, etc. Each video was rib- tickling and humorous. I immediately subscribed to his YouTube channel.

THREE

"Oh Harry! Why do we need to make these silly projects?" Sameer and I were sitting in his room at his house. It was our autumn break and we had to complete our first Economics project. I brought my pens, pencils and other stuff to his house. The Desi Dude wasn't interested in making the project.

"We have to complete it soon; otherwise the project will become a burden for us later," I replied.

"Only cowards do projects and assignments early. Brave people like me complete such stuff a night before the deadline."

"Desi Dude, we have already chatted a lot. Let's focus on the project," I said sternly.

"Okay okay Harry sir," he replied in a meek voice.

Both of us started making the project. We were sitting on his bed and we filled its surface with sketch pens, pencil shavings, papers, refills, etc. Suddenly, Sameer started looking for something.

"Hey, I think I left my stencil in the other room. Let me bring it here. Bro, you wait for me."

"Okay Desi Dude."

He went out of the room. In the meantime, I decided to look around his room. The walls were filled with photos of various comedians like Raju Srivastava, Sunil Pal, Ehsaan Qureshi, and many others that I didn't know. There was a poster of AIB on the door of a cupboard. There was another picture of Sameer himself performing on the stage and 'DESI DUDE' was written as a caption on the photo. Thus, his room looked like a studio rather than a place for studies.

He returned to the room with the stencil.

"Sorry bro. I forgot where it was kept. So I got late," Sameer said.

"Hey Sam, I was looking around your room. Your room is interesting. The walls look elegant with the posters."

"Oh thanks. These posters are my buddies as well as my inspiration. I have collected them from various places."

"Bro, you are born for comedy."

"I also think so. I don't want to pursue studies. I don't love studies. By the way, you were chiding me for focusing on the project. Now you have started blabbering," he back fired my words on me.

We again started working on our projects. After some time, Sameer's mother entered the room. She was a thin lady. She was wearing a light coloured saree and was holding a tray.

"Hey boys. Take a break from your work. I have prepared tea and *lithi chokha* for you."

"*Lithi chokha*! I ate it a long time ago at my grandmother's house in Kanpur. I loved its taste," I exclaimed in joy.

"Oh nice. Sameer told me that you are also from UP. So I prepared it for both of you. Sameer loves to eat it."

"Thank you aunty ji," I said in joy.

"Thank you mom," Sameer said.

"Welcome boys. But remember, please do clean up the mess you have created on the bed," she said sternly.

"Okay aunty ji."

She nodded and left the room. Sameer turned to me.

"My mom prepares delicious *lithi chokha*. I hope you will also love it."

We ate the food prepared by his mom. It was really very delicious. The tea was ginger tea and it was tasty too. After eating it, we again resumed the project work. We worked on it for two hours.

"Oh we have completed enough of the project. Now we should complete the remaining part later," I said.

"You are right bro," he said after taking a sigh of relief.

We cleaned the bed and I packed up my stationery and other stuff.

"So, we will meet at Raghav sir's class. Tell aunty ji that the *lithi chokha* and the tea were very tasty."

"Okay bro."

I left his house. The posters of various comedians and comedy shows were still flashing in front of my eyes. Sameer didn't like academics and he wanted to make his career in comedy. He was a guy who wanted to go against the flow.

It was the last day of our autumn break. I departed from my home to Sameer's home for completing the remaining portion of our assignment. As I was about to reach his house, I heard loud yells from inside the house.

"This brat has troubled me. He is never serious about his

studies. Look at his marks. The children of my colleagues are school toppers. Most of them have got admission either in IITs or reputed colleges of the Delhi University. "

"Dear, please forgive him. I will talk to him." A female voice came from the house, which I assumed to be his mother's.

"You have been saying this since last six years. I am fed up of this brat since he took arts instead of science in class eleventh. Though I am going through a severe financial crisis, I have gone beyond my means for his education. But he is just ignorant..."

I could guess the topic of the heated argument. I found that retreating from that place would be a better option. As I was leaving, the door of Sameer's house banged open. He came out of his house hurriedly and saw me. Though he had an intense fight with his father, his expression did not show that. He was looking as jolly as he looked at other times.

"Sameer, I will come some other day. I can understand..."

"Hey Harry, it does not matter. It is the daily drama of my house. Just ignore. Let's just hang out."

We came to the Prashant Vihar Park for a walk. As we were walking, I could not decide what to speak to him. After a few minutes, I gathered courage and asked him-

"Sam, your father was talking about some financial crisis. If you do not mind, can you share about it?"

Sameer stopped for a while. His face turned expressionless. I thought I had asked something wrong. I got scared. But he again resumed walking and started telling his story.

"I have an elder brother, Nitish Mishra. He is six years older to me. He did graduation from the Delhi University and then he wanted to do MBA. He got admission in a private institute. My father took a loan of fifteen lakh rupees for the course. My father was the guarantor of the loan. But when he completed the course and got a job in Chennai through campus placement, he refused to repay the debt. Father requested him every time to at least give a portion of the loan, but his heart did not melt. Now he has changed his mobile number. We do not even know what he is doing now, where he is staying, etc. We do not have any contact with him since one year."

Though he was speaking such an intense thing, his face remained jolly.

"Oh Gosh. So why didn't uncle ji take any legal steps against your brother to recover the money?"

"Actually my father is highly concerned about his self-esteem. He did not want to engage police or courts into the matter as it could tarnish our family's reputation in front of our relatives and his colleagues. So he silently resorted to paying the debt himself. "

Sameer belonged to a middle class family like me. His father was an upper division clerk at some Central Government office and his mother was a housewife. Delhi is one of the most expensive cities in India. The prices of the commodities are soaring, so savings is very difficult for middle class people.

"Fifteen lakh rupees. It is a huge sum. I would say you should start working hard for your studies, so that you can get a good job and help your father."

"Harry, you are also repeating my father's words. I know studying can provide me a good job with a good salary. But what's the logic behind pursuing a path which I don't like. I can understand my father's condition, but how can I sacrifice my desire, dreams and aspirations for my entire life. If I become a successful stand-up comedian, then also I can financially help him. As I said earlier, I am adamant about it."

His argument was also strong. I did not have any argument to counter his viewpoint.

"I can only say that the path you want to pursue is full of challenges," it was the only thing I could say.

I found that the atmosphere was becoming very intense, so I diverted the conversation from this issue.

"So Sam, why don't you try in the comedy shows that are aired on the television? They can give you a platform to showcase your talent."

"Ya I agree, but in a nutshell I can say that I do not like their format. Their format has become mundane. I want to do something new. I want to 'redefine' comedy."

"Ya, but that's next to impossible for laymen like us."

"You don't worry. I will make that possible."

Sameer truly had a great dream. But I found that his dream was not supported by any action plan or agenda. Though he had great talent, he wasn't sure about how to proceed towards achieving his aspirations. The main problem was his family itself.

FOUR

It was the month of December. We had a routine class at the Success House. But that time, four of us decided to meet near the institute after our class as we didn't go for any scooty rides after we were shuffled into different batches. The class got over and Sameer and I came out of the class. Himanshu and Nitin were waiting for us on their scooty.

"So, let's go for a ride, bro," Himanshu grinned.

I sat behind Himanshu and Sameer sat behind Nitin. They rode at high speed through various colonies. Then we came on the outer Ring Road and then on the GT Karnal Road. It was a vacant highway.

"Hey guys, I think we should now return," I spoke as loudly as possible, but my voice was inaudible to them at such a high speed.

As we reached the Delhi border, Himanshu and Nitin realised that they had come very far from our houses.

"Let's return guys. We have come too far," Himanshu said.

It was December and four of us were feeling very cold. The

road got covered with fog. Nitin and Himanshu were facing difficulty in driving the scooty. Suddenly, Sameer spoke out.

"Hey guys, there are some farms along the road. Let's stop here and light a fire."

Both of them stopped their respective scooties near a farm. We collected some wooden sticks for lighting the fire. Sameer spotted a local paan shop and he bought a matchbox.

We lit the fire and sat around it. We were enjoying its heat.

"Hey guys, I remember a shayari after seeing this fire."

Lakriyo mein jo aag lagti hai, woh paani se bujh jaati hai,

Lakriyo mein jo aag lagti hai, woh paani se bujh jaati hai

Lekin jo aag tum dil mein lagati ho, woh koi fire brigade bhi bujha nahi pati hai.

We started laughing. He presented many other shayaris, which we loved to hear. He also told many jokes. It seemed that we were sitting around a bonfire in a cold night and enjoying the moment.

Suddenly our phones started ringing. Our parents were calling.

"Hey guys, I think we should leave now. It's 10 pm. Our parents will be very angry."

"Yes yes. Let's move," I said.

The fire slowly disappeared. We sat on the scooties and Himanshu and Nitin drove us back to our homes. We were anxious about our parent's reaction when they would see us. We were thinking about various excuses like extra classes, stay back, surprise test, etc.

When I entered my house, I found that dad was sitting on the drawing room's sofa. He looked at me as I entered.

"Harish, I am noticing that you are spending a lot of time with your friends. Don't forget that your exams are nearing. I think I do not need to say anything else."

"Dad, I will now focus on my studies."

"Child, you will have ample time after your board exams to spend with your friends. Now you set your priorities. If you need any kind of help from us, feel free to tell us."

I would say that my father's leniency was more powerful than someone's scolding. Whenever he said anything to me leniently, no power could stop me from following it. My parents were very supportive. They never pressurised me for studies. They always motivated me and whenever they found that I was going on a wrong track, they warned me.

December was over and it was January. I attended my Saturday's class at the Success Point and returned to my home. I did not hang out with Himanshu and Nitin to keep my word to my father. The exams were two months away. Sameer didn't attend the class.

After returning home, I had a supper and sat down to revise the notes of Raghav sir. An hour later, my phone started ringing. It was Sameer's call. I picked up the call.

"Harry, did you attend today's class?"

"Yes Sam. Why didn't you attend the class?"

"Actually I called you for that only. Tomorrow, I have a performance at Aloha Lounge. It is a 'Conti' party of my school. The Head Boy of our school is organising it and he requested me to perform out there. I want you to come with me tomorrow, so that you can see my live performance. He is my close friend and he will not charge us any fees. The programme is in evening and we can depart together. "

Lounges were a new trend in Delhi. They were mushrooming rapidly there. Secondly, the Conti party also became a new 'custom' for the twelfth standard students.

"Ya but I have never visited a lounge before."

"Hey, don't worry; things will be fine out there. I will be happy if you accompany me. I also asked Himanshu and Nitin, but both of them can't come."

"But my parents..."

"Just make an excuse to them, like extra classes, test, etc. It's my earnest request. I want you in the audience to witness my performance."

His way of requesting melted my heart.

"Okay I will try. I will inform you by tomorrow morning."

"Yes, please bro."

Next day I woke up a bit early. I straightened the bed sheet and kept the pillows at their places. Suddenly my mother entered the room.

"Hari beta, today there is a 'jagrata' at one of your father's colleague's house in the evening. We will return around midnight. I will prepare your dinner before leaving. You just warm it yourself before eating it."

I thought that fate also wants me to see Sameer's live performance. I knew that attending the party would mean demeaning the words given to my father. But I could not dishonour Sameer's earnest request too. So I took the midway. I studied heavily in the morning and the afternoon, so that I could easily attend the show.

I called Sameer to inform him. He was very happy. We decided to depart for the lounge at 6 pm and decided that we will try to return by 11 pm.

My parents left for the 'jagrata' at 4pm. Sameer walked to my house at 5.30 pm. Both of us took an auto-rickshaw and reached the Aloha Lounge on time. The lounge was full of twelfth standard students of Kendriya Vidyalaya. I did not know any of them. They understood that I was the one who came with Sameer. I was also feeling very nervous because I came to a lounge for the first time. I never saw a place before with dim light and a counter full of different drinks.

In a few minutes, the Head Boy of the school took a microphone and started speaking.

"Aloha guys. As you all know, I have invited your favourite comedian, Sameer Sam."

The crowd shouted 'yeah' as they heard his name. The Head Boy continued.

"But before calling Sameer on the stage, I want you all to welcome a guest to our 'Conti'. He is the guy sitting at the corner of the room"

I guessed that he was talking about me.

"He is Sameer's close friend and he is Harish Harry. Please welcome him."

The crowd looked at me and started clapping and hooting. I felt shy.

Eventually, Sameer came to the stage. He was wearing a loose blue T-shirt, jeans and black goggles. His thin body with pointed beard and such apparel made him look very funny.

At first, he gave a very hilarious introduction. Then he mocked some teachers of his school. He also pointed out the famous couples of his batch who had attended the party and made fun of them. He also emphasised how a Desi guy proposes a city girl and what happens after that. The crowd kept laughing. There was hardly any second in which they stopped their laughter. He ended the performance with a funny rap song. The rap was on how a Desi guy dates a city girl. The audience kept laughing even after he finished his performance. It was a great performance.

Sameer first came to me and asked about his performance. I didn't have words to appreciate him. We ate our snacks at the party. He introduced me to his friends. I met new people and was enjoying myself, but I had resolved to reach home by 11pm. Sameer wanted to stay there longer as well but as he was committed to me to reach home by 11, we started at 10.30 pm from the lounge. I reached home at exactly 11 pm.

"Thanks Sam for the wonderful night," I said.

"No I thank you for coming with me. I wanted you to see my performance live instead of the recorded performance."

"So meet you at the weekly test at the Success Point. Goodbye Sam."

"Good night Harry," he said and left for his home.

I unlocked the door and entered the house. Luckily, mom and dad hadn't returned. I ate the food cooked by my mother and laid on my bed. I was recalling each moment I spent at the lounge, where I first time saw Sameer's performance live.

FIVE

Raghav sir had kept a test on a Sunday for three hours. I reached the centre and gave the test. As I was leaving after submitting the answer sheet, I saw Sameer standing with a man, whom I guessed was his father and Raghav sir. Sameer's head was bowed down. Since the exit gate was through a narrow corridor, where three of them were standing. I couldn't dare to ask them to shift, so I waited till they left and as a result, I heard their conversation.

"Rakesh ji, your son has skipped many of my tests without any valid reasons. He scores very less marks in the tests that he gave. His attendance in my class is poor and he hasn't attended even a single extra class that I have kept so far."

"Sir I really don't know what to do with this boy. He is never interested in studies. Though his performance in academics has been very poor since a very long time, he does not have any shame or repentance. I am fed up of this moron. I am working very hard to pay for his schooling and coaching. I have gone almost beyond my means. But this brat never understands. He is very stubborn. Sir, I am totally helpless..."

Uncle ji was about to break down.

"Sir, don't worry. The Economics exam is still two months away. You at least tell Sameer to revise my notes. It will help him to score at least above 70%."

His father did not speak even a word and left. Sameer followed him with a bowed head. I felt very bad for both of them.

It was the month of February and only a month was left for the exams. Sameer came to my house to click photos of the notes, which were given in the classes that he didn't attend.

"Harry bro, the concepts of demand and supply are so complicated! I am unable to grasp any of them," he said in a nasty tone.

"Yes I can understand, Sam...," I said.

"Oh my God. So many diagrams in micro and macro eco, and formulae too," he said.

"Just learn those portions that you find easy. I can understand," I said.

"You can understand, my friends can understand, my teachers can understand, why my dad can't understand?" he said in anger. I understood that he was pointing towards the lack of support from his dad for becoming a stand-up comedian.

"See, Uncle ji is also right. At least the boards..."

"I think you are my dad's counterpart, Harry. I told you as well as him that I was never interested in studies. If others say that I have some skills, why shouldn't I follow it? If the studies are burden for me at this stage, then the graduation level studies will just crush me!"

"Well…"

"Hey Harry, are we participating in any debate competition? We have started arguing on such a silly issue," he changed the topic.

"But you are the one who started this argument," I said.

"Well, whatever. Show me the macro notes," he said jokingly.

I took out the macro notes from the cupboard. He looked at the notes with a pitiful face. He took their snapshots in his mobile phone.

"Hey Harry, let's go out to have momos in the evening," Sameer said.

"No bro, I have to study English literature," I replied.

"English! People study English a day before exam. Just skip your studies for a day."

"No bro, next time, for sure," I said.

"Okay then next time."

He departed from my house. I started studying English.

Finally the board exams started and I stopped receiving phone calls from Sameer, Himanshu and Nitin. The exams were going well, with a lot of preparation leaves between each exam. The exam days were rigorous.

Finally the exams got over in the mid of April. I became a free bird. Sameer, Himanshu, Nitin and I would roam here and there on their scooties. We also used to go to see Sameer's comedy shows. He called himself 'The Desi Dude.' His performances were mind-blowing.

One day I started chatting with Sameer on personal chat.

"Hi Sam, what's up?"

"Hey Harry, I am eating Maggi at my home."

"Eating Maggi alone. I also want to eat it."

"Poor joke. He he..."

"He he…"

"So have you decided anything for your career?"

"Yes, I want to pursue law."

"Law! But you can easily get admission in Delhi University."

"I found that law will be suitable for me as a career. I have already applied for CLAT."

"So have you started preparing for it?"

"Ya, I took a book from my cousin for preparation. I am practicing the questions from the book."

"Nice dude."

"What about you, Desi comedian?"

"Ya I want to pursue my dream, but I don't know how to proceed. My family, especially my father will not allow my dreams to get fulfilled."

"Let's hope for the best."

"Yes Harry bhai."

"☺ ☺"

Sameer and I used to meet at the Prashant Vihar Park for evening walks. We did jogging together and hanged out after jogging.

SIX

I practised the questions from my cousin's book. Gradually the day of the CLAT arrived. I went to the exam centre and gave the test. The exam went well. Now I was waiting for both the CLAT result and 12th board result.

It had been around four weeks that I did not have any contact with anyone except the Desi Dude. I was sure that all my friends were anxious about their results. The Board result and the CLAT result were declared almost simultaneously. I had scored 94% in class 12th board and got rank 125 in CLAT. My parents allowed me to pursue law as my career.

I was getting admission at the Maharashtra National Law University, Mumbai. I also came to know that Himanshu was getting admission at The Bhartiya Vidyapeeth, Pune in BJMC. Nitin got admission at the Motilal Nehru College in History Honours. I didn't ask Sameer's marks. However, I whatsapped him about my admission at MNLU. He sent me the symbol of 'like'.

One day, I received a call from Sameer at 8 pm.

"Harry, can you please come to meet me at the District Park? It's very urgent."

"Now?"

"Yes, please."

Sameer was sounding desperate. I quickly changed my dress, wore my shoes and proceeded to the park. I saw him sitting on a bench. As I went near him, I saw that his face looked tense. I could not understand what happened to him.

"Hey, Desi Dude, why are you looking so tense today?"

"I don't know where to start from, dude."

"Is anything wrong?" I asked him although I knew where he was indicating.

"Harry, I have scored 59% in the Board exam. My father was very furious. Earlier he at least scolded me, but now he has stopped talking to me. However today, he badly blasted out. Instead of chiding me, he started speaking harshly to my mother in front of me."

"You dirty lady! You are responsible for giving birth to brats. You witch!"

"I tried my best to teach them..." She started sobbing. She never spoke loudly in front of my dad.

"And 59% is the outcome of your teaching! He has just insulted me, like your elder son. Now no university will give him admission!" He raised his hand to slap my mom, but I instantly grasped his raised hand firmly to stop him.

"How dare you do this to my mother? If you have a problem with me, scold me, not her."

I could not control my anger and I picked up a flower vase and broke it at his feet. I can tolerate anything spoken to me, but I cannot tolerate even a single harsh word spoken to my mother.

"Like your elder brother, you are no more my son. Just get lost from here. Just do whatever you want. I don't care anymore."

I just ran away from my house and I just don't want to return there. Dad is a very arrogant person. He is only concerned about his 'fictitious' fame and reputation. Such feeling has suppressed my happiness. His dirty frustration comes not from the debt trap but from the feelings he develops when his colleagues brag in front of him about their children.

Tears started rolling out of his eyes as he was telling me about it. But he stopped his tears within a few seconds and resumed the conversation. I was dumbstruck.

"My dad always says, 'Sharma ji's son did this', 'Sharma ji's son won that prize' and bla bla bla. I have never seen either that Sharma ji or his idiotic son. I know many Delhiite dads speak about Sharma ji's son. But have you ever wondered, who is the bloody Sharma ji and his buffoonish son."

"Yes. You are right."

Sameer took a deep breath.

"Harry, I want to go to Mumbai along with you."

I gathered courage to speak something to him.

"That's fine. But what will you do in Mumbai? As you know, I am going there for studies."

"I will go there to trouble you and shake hands with Alia Bhat," he giggled.

I didn't know how he can take himself out of a tense mood so quickly.

"What?"

"Just kidding. As I told you about my troop, it is linked with an agency, which has a branch in Mumbai. The agency wanted a stand-up comedian and the troop recommended my name. I not only want to pursue my career in comedy but want to elope from my house. My house is not a house, it is Germany's concentration camp."

"Ya that's nice. But God forbid, if the agency thing doesn't work out, then you will be completely alone in a huge city."

"Bro, I will work as a daily wager or sell newspapers, but I don't want to come back to my house. The atmosphere at my home will not only ruin my comedy skills but also my life. We will stay together in a rented room and share our expenses. My mother said that she will try to send me some money every month. Please, it's my request. Please bro."

"I don't have any issues. I will be glad if you come with me."

"And Harry, do you know what my dad use to say when he scolds me?"

"What, Sam?"

"My dad says that if I don't study and get a good job, he will not be able to demand a hefty dowry from the bride's family for the marriage!"

"What? Dowry!" I was shocked to hear that a person was talking about dowry in the twenty-first century.

"Oh Harry! Actually my village is still backward and some evil practices, like dowry are still present there. The dowry amount is fixed according to the job of the groom. For instance, an IAS officer, IITian engineer or a doctor gets the highest dowry, a professor of any public university or a police officer gets the second level of dowry, a government school teacher or a Grade C officer gets the third level and so on."

I was sure that my dad didn't take any dowry from my mom's family as both of them belonged to a modern and progressive family. I was afraid of asking Sameer whether his dad took any dowry for marrying his mother. He continued-

"Don't think that I will demand for any dowry. I totally condemn it. So have you booked your ticket for Mumbai?"

"I will book a ticket in Delhi-Mumbai Rajdhani Express in the Tatkal quota. I will depart for Mumbai on 5th June."

"Book two tickets. We will go together. I will pay you the ticket charges."

"Okay sure."

"But now, where will you go?"

"I will tolerate the atmosphere till 5th June. Today is 29th May. It's a matter of few days. I am sure my mother will support me. When I came to know that you are going to Mumbai for law, I decided to accompany you there to escape from my house, from my dad."

"Okay sure."

"Another thing, I wish I were born to your parents. At least I would have got support since my childhood to pursue my comedy career. I could have honed my skill right from my home. I am jealous of you bro in this matter."

I felt proud of my parents. We decided what to take with us for the journey. I wanted to stay in the MNLU hostel, but it was okay for me to stay with Sameer in a PG. It will save some of my expenses. Plus staying in an unknown city with a known person will be advantageous for me.

After pacifying Sameer, I returned to my home and told my parents about his request. My parents were delighted as I will have a known companion in an unknown city. My father booked our tickets through the Tatkal quota in the New Delhi-Mumbai Rajdhani Express. Luckily, our seats were together, B6 26 and 27. Sameer gave me the charges of his ticket in cash. I was, thus, excited that I will get a nice companion in the new phase of my life.

SEVEN

I had packed my bags. I kept all the certificates, mark sheets, clothes and other requirements for Mumbai. I also kept a family photograph in my bag. My parents helped me to pack the things properly. Both of them were upset because they had spent so many years with me and I was leaving them for my higher studies.

It was 4th June, a day before our departure to Mumbai. As my father went out for a while, my mother came to my room and gave me a bundle of cash.

"Hari beta, this is for emergency purpose and contingencies. Use these carefully. I have saved this money from the household budget."

I hugged her tightly. I was about to cry. I did not want to leave her. After the bag was packed, mother went to the kitchen to cook our dinner. I was sitting on my bed and was recalling whether I had taken all necessary things or not. Suddenly, my concentration was broken by the ringing of my phone. As I took my mobile, I saw that it was an unknown number. I picked the call.

"Hello," I said.

"Hello. Am I talking to Harish?"

It was a hoarse voice, probably of a middle-aged man.

"Yes, I am Harish speaking."

"I am Mr. Rakesh, Sameer's father."

I was gasping. I had never talked to Sameer's father before. His voice was desperate, which made me more nervous.

"Namaste uncle ji."

"Namaste beta. I came to know that Sameer is going along with you to Mumbai."

"Yes uncle ji. The train is tomorrow at 4 pm. New Delhi-Mumbai Rajdhani."

"See, what he will do there, where he will go, I really don't care. But I want a promise from you."

"Yes uncle ji."

"Beta, I have earned very less money throughout my life, but I have earned a huge reputation. Wherever he will go, he will carry my fame and reputation. I don't want my only possession, which is my reputation, to get shattered by any of his wrong conduct."

"Yes uncle ji," I answered in a meek voice.

"You promise me that you will protect my fame and reputation as I have lost my faith and trust on that character. You try your best to abstain him from doing any wrong thing."

"I promise uncle. I will try my best."

"I am telling all this to you because I will not go to the railway station tomorrow. Don't tell him and his mother about whatever I told you just now. I trust you."

"Yes, sure, uncle ji."

"Thank you, dear. Good luck, Harish beta. Happy journey. Good night."

He ended the call. I was left stunned for a few moments. Then I thought that if uncle ji would have told 'Good Luck' to Sameer at least once in his lifetime, he would have become a famous stand up comedian instantly. He would have found himself the happiest person on the earth. When I recalled his dialogue about his fame, I could feel Sameer's anguish which he was sharing at the District Park. But as I promised him to be vigilant about the acts of Sameer, I will try to keep it.

Now the D-Day arrived- 5th June. My mother woke up before me to complete the eleventh hour works. My father went to his office, but he would take a half-day leave and come to home before 2 pm. Sameer and I had already planned that we will hire two auto rickshaws for going to the station. He went to the auto stand near our home and asked two auto drivers to come to pick us at 2 pm sharp. My mother kept wafers, chips, chocolates and fruits in my bag for the journey although I told her that we get adequate food at regular intervals in the Rajdhani Express.

My father returned home at 1.50 pm. The autos arrived at 2 pm sharp. I saw that Sameer and his mother were already sitting in one of the autos. Dad, mom and I kept our luggage in the bonnet of the other one and sat in it. Luckily we got less traffic jam on the way and we reached the New Delhi railway station at 3.15 pm. Five of us were waiting on the platform for the train. Dad got a phone call from his office and he went at the other side of the platform to take it. I started chatting with Sameer about the things that we have packed. In the meantime, the two ladies also started talking.

"Hello sister, what is your name?" said my mother.

"I am Rani Mishra. What is your name?" said his mother.

"I am Kusum Shukla. Sameer used to come to our house for notes and assignments. By the way, why didn't bhaiya ji come?"

My mother didn't know the background of the entire tale. So she asked such a controversial question. Even Sameer's mother got silent for a while, but she continued.

"Actually Sameer's father did not get a leave today. So he could not come."

"Ya I can understand. Harish's father also wanted a full day leave today. But he managed to get only a half day," my mother replied innocently.

"Okay, Kusum behen. So, where are you from UP?"

"My maiden house is in Jaunpur. My in-laws stay in Kanpur. What about you?"

"My maiden house and Sameer's father's house are both in Balia. One of my cousins stays in Jaunpur."

"Oh nice. I am so excited that our sons will start a new phase of life together. Rani behen, I am a bit nervous how will they tackle everything?"

"Don't worry. Our boys are smart enough. They will manage. By the way, please give me your contact number."

"Yes, save it. Please give me a call in this number so that I can save it."

Both of them saved each other's numbers and in the meantime, the train arrived at the platform. We entered into our compartment and reached our reserved seats. Our parents helped us to keep our luggage under the seats. Then they gave us the last minute instructions and advices. They got down from the compartment five minutes before the departure time of the train. It started leaving the station at its scheduled time. Sameer and I saw our parents from the window waving at us. They looked very sad.

As the train gained pace, I also felt upset because I was going away from my parents for the first time. Sameer looked at me.

"Hey Harry, do you remember our Head Boy whom you saw at our Conti?" He was trying to divert my mind from the dilemma.

"Yes, I remember."

"Do you know there is a funny tale about him?"

"Ya tell me."

Sameer started narrating the tale. It was a bit derogatory although it was very funny. Then he continued to narrate hilarious incidents at his school, which were truly rib-tickling. Then he also read the funny 'shayaris' that he composed himself. He was making the journey interesting. I almost forgot all the sorrows and tensions. Even our co-passengers were enjoying his jokes and 'shayaris'. At night before going to sleep, I again started pondering about the thing to be done in Mumbai, counselling at MNLU, finding a nice PG, etc.

It is the turning point of the story. Sameer and I were entering into a new world together. The new world was in Mumbai, the 'Mayapuri', or the 'Land of Dreams', in terms of academics as well as non-academic career. The years spent by me there were truly memorable.

EIGHT

Nine years ago, Mumbai

We reached Mumbai Central station at the scheduled time. The journey was awesome. Sameer and I carried our luggage to the taxi-stand. We hired a taxi and asked him to take us to different PGs and hostels, so that we can get an affordable one. While travelling in the taxi, we were looking at the streets of Mumbai. The street was full of hustle and bustle. We enjoyed travelling through the Marine Drive. We saw Siddhi Vinayak, Haji Ali Dargah and the Gateway of India on the way. We found the city unique as we had been staying in New Delhi for a long time.

"Wow, what a beautiful city!" I said while travelling in the taxi.

"Yes. It's a lovely city," Sameer said.

"Now let's find a nice and affordable PG for us," I said.

"Yes. But we will miss momos, chole bhature, etc. in Mumbai," he grinned.

We checked five PGs and finally we selected the sixth one, which was in Powai. I saw that Sameer was very good at bargaining. The room had only one window and one attached bathroom. There were two single beds, one almirah and one study table. It was on the terrace of the landlord. There was a kitchen on the other side of the terrace, which had an old refrigerator. We selected it because it was nearer to MNLU, a beautiful park and the market. We kept our luggage in the room and called our parents. They were very excited.

We went out to have our lunch. Then we returned to the room, and rested for some time. Then I started putting my credentials to be produced during the counselling in a folder. We again went out in the evening to purchase our daily provisions like vegetables, oil, spices, mosquito repellents, etc. The counselling was the next day. Sameer was also supposed to meet the agency people the next day.

Next day the alarm awoke us at 7 am. We got ready together and departed for our respective destinations. I entered the MNLU campus. At that time, it was a newly established law university. It was a huge campus. I went to the auditorium where the counselling was taking place. Various professors of the university came and explained the course details, rules and regulations, code of conduct, etc. I made many friends at the counselling session, who remained my friends throughout the course. One of them was from Vasant Kunj, New Delhi and others were from different places in Maharashtra. After the session, my new friends and I probed the campus. It was like a new world on the earth.

I returned to my room in the afternoon. I was so excited that I forgot to cook the lunch. Sameer also returned after an hour. I was so excited that as he entered the room, I caught him and started narrating my experience at the MNLU, without even asking for his experience.

"Harry dude first let me breathe."

"Breathe later on Sam, first let me complete. And you know, the guy from Vasant Kunj said…" I was completing the statement when Sameer interrupted.

"Okay okay I understand your excitement. Calm down. I will listen to you patiently a bit later."

I controlled my temptations and allowed him to relax. In the meantime, I went to the kitchen to prepare the lunch. As we were eating, I again started narrating my tale. As he promised, he listened to each and every thing very patiently. Then I asked him to tell his experience. He started.

"I took the visiting card which I brought from Delhi. I changed buses and finally reached the office. The name of the office was Naval Entertainment Pvt. Ltd, Andheri East. I met the manager, whose name was Anil Shinde. He was a short, fat and grumpy man. He had a huge tummy…"

"Ya I have heard about you. The Desi Dude from Delhi. Arora recommended you to me," he said while chuckling.

"Yes sir," I said.

"See as per the policy of our company, we will first audition you. Then we shall send you wherever there will be a requirement for a comedian. If you are found suitable in that performance, then we will send you further. But you will not receive any remuneration for your first show."

"Okay sir."

"Ha, there are many stand-up comedians in the queue. People crave to work for Shinde. But as Arora has recommended you, let's test you. I have ten years experience. I can turn a 'nothing' into a celebrity. There are lakhs of YouTube comedians in this country. Booo" he grinned.

"I didn't find him a genial person, but still I showed him some of my videos on my cell phone. He sounded very arrogant and like a psycho. He told me to fill a form and come day after tomorrow for an audition."

"Sam, so what have you thought?" I asked him.

"See, first of all I will give audition at that psycho's office. Then I will prepare my next agenda as per the circumstances," he replied. His way of talking showed that he was not much convinced in his first meeting.

NINE

Sameer's audition was a day before the commencement of my classes at the MNLU. He cooked and ate his breakfast and left for the audition. He prepared himself the whole night for it. He returned in the evening to the room and that day, he was looking excited. I assumed that there was good news.

"So Desi Dude, what's the news?"

He first entered the room, drank a glass of water and then started.

"I reached the office on time. There were many other people who came for the audition. When I entered into the room, the judges gave me a piece of paper in the audition in which certain statements were written. Shinde was also sitting there. They asked me to read out the lines in the funniest way I could. The audition was quite difficult as the sentences didn't have any funny element in them. However I managed to read it in funny way. The judges asked me to wait outside along with the other contestants."

Sameer took a pause. The pause that he took was at such an interesting juncture that I couldn't resist my temptation to hear the rest of the story.

"Sam please continue quickly, I can't wait."

"Calm down calm down. I am continuing."

"As the auditions were over, Shinde came out of the room after fifteen minutes. He was carrying a sheet of paper. He started making his declaration-

"The judges have selected five 'nothings' as comedians for my firm. I want those five 'nothings' to stay back while others may leave. The five lucky names are Rahul Kashyap, Paras Kumar, Akshay Malangkar, Keshav Tawre and Sameer Mishra."

"Wow congratulations Sam ji, the Desi Dude. Kudos"

"Thanks Harry bhai. Then as five of us stayed back, he allotted us our first shows. I have to perform at the unofficial Annual day party of the employees of the Yes Bank. Shinde asked us to reach the places on time. He also asked me separately to give up my name 'Sameer Mishra' and adopt the new name - the Desi Dude forever."

"Oh nice!"

"So Harry, the performance is on coming Sunday. I want you to witness my first performance in Mumbai. No ifs and buts, only a yes."

"Okay bro. I will go with you," I said.

"The next thing we need to do is to buy vegetables from the market for today's dinner and tomorrow's lunch."

"Hey Sam, again jokes."

"I am no more Sam. Now I am Desi Dude, mohahahaha...," he sounded like a Raavan of Delhi's Ramleela.

We purchased vegetables and rice from the market for the dinner. I used to talk to my parents and Sameer, sorry the Desi Dude, to his mother regularly. Our contact with Himanshu and Nitin diminished gradually as they got busy in their new lives. In between I came to know that the Desi Dude's father was suffering from high blood pressure. His mother was very anxious about his father's health.

My first class at MNLU was fantastic. I sat with those people whom I met in the counselling. Sameer was preparing for his first performance in Mumbai. So our PG room became a spot of diverse activities. He used to go to the Naval Entertainment Pvt. Ltd. frequently.

It was Sunday. Sameer woke up very early, although the event was in the evening, for his final practice. He did not make much noise, which was advantageous for me. The event was at Savitri Bai Phule Hall, Nariman Point. Both of us departed in the afternoon for it. As we reached there, we saw Shinde standing at the entrance.

"Shinde ji, he is my friend, Harish."

He looked exactly the same as Sameer described earlier-short, fat, grumpy with a huge tummy.

"Hello beta. You take a seat in the hall. Both of us will be at the back stage."

I entered the hall. I saw that the employees came in traditional dresses, where the male staff wore sherwani and female staff wore elegant sarees. They were looking very jolly and it seemed that they were gossiping about their superiors. Someone told that it was a private party of the employees, where the top level managers were not invited. A volunteer, who was a young employee of the bank, ushered me to a corner seat. I sat on the seat and looked at the decoration of the stage and the lighting of the hall. After a few minutes, an anchor, who was also an employee of the bank, asked everyone to take the seats as the show was about to begin.

The show started with sarcastic comments on the grumpy seniors. The audience could not control their laughter. Then few young personnel prepared a small skit and dance performance to show the dreadful life of a private sector employee. Then another employee came and announced the funny titles given to different employees as per their personality. The titles made the employees happy. Finally the anchor came to the stage and made an announcement.

"Now it's time for the show for which everyone has been waiting eagerly. It's the time for the Comedy Night. Now the wait is over. Mr. Anil Shinde presents in front of you a young desi comedian- The Desi Dude!"

The audience started hooting and clapping loudly. It showed that the employees knew about Sameer's comedy show. The stage lights were dimmed for a few seconds, which left the audience perplexed. Then suddenly the lights were made bright and he came to the stage wearing a T- shirt, white dhoti and black goggles. He had a dark moustache and thick beard. He was looking very funny and the audience started laughing just by seeing him.

"Hi brothers and their sisters. I am your Desi Dude," he gave his introduction in his desi tone. The audience again started laughing.

Sameer started his performance with 'shayaris' on the lives of employees and the strictness of the managers. He then changed the topic and started narrating the experiences of a village boy in an urban area, where he sees various ironies. He also mocked at the tantrums of city girls, short lived love affairs at schools and colleges, the unending demands of the girlfriends, etc. The employees could not stop their laughter and after each joke, they were yelling "Once more, once more." I saw Shinde standing with the organisers of the event and was grinning. Sameer ended his performance with a medley of parody song in which he criticised the domineering managers who put loads of tasks on the employee's shoulders and then he left the stage.

The audience stood up and clapped for a long time. Some of them kept laughing. The organisers were shaking hands with Shinde. The anchor again came to the stage and appreciated the performance of the Desi Dude. Then she asked the audience to proceed to the adjacent hall for dinner. As I was leaving the hall, the employees whom I confronted were appreciating Sameer's talent and sense of humour. I felt proud to have a friend like him. I met Sameer at the dinner hall.

"Harry, how was my performance?"

"Awesome bro. You just set the stage on fire."

"Oh thanks bro."

The employees came to him and appreciated his talent. He was blushing when a group of female employees, who were in their early twenties, came to him and started taking photographs with him. Even I felt a bit jealous of him.

After the dinner, both of us started leaving the auditorium, when Shinde stopped us.

"You Sam ji, your performance was not bad. Still a 'nothing' performance. You remember the terms and conditions of my firm, don't you?"

"Yes sir. No payment for the first performance."

"Good my child. One of the organisers who stay in Powai has been helpful enough to drop you at your PG. You, the Desi one, meet me tomorrow at my office so that we can decide your future with my firm."

Shinde truly spoke in a very harsh way. Though we could have gone to our PG ourselves, he made us believe that the organiser was doing us a huge favour. I thought that Sameer was in very harsh hands.

The organiser dropped us to our PG. We thanked him and entered our room. Sameer was very exhausted.

TEN

Next day, Sameer left for Shinde's office early in the morning. I also got ready and left for MNLU. It was a day full of lectures. We had classes on mercantile laws, environmental laws, Corporate Law and Bare Acts. After the classes, I hanged out with my friends at MNLU to refresh our minds. We ate our lunch at the canteen and then left for our PGs.

As I entered the room, I found Sameer lying on the bed awake.

"Hey Sam, how was your encounter with Shinde?"

"Hmmm."

"Hey!"

"Huh, I went straight to his office today. I entered into Shinde's cabin."

"You Desi guy, the committee found your act nice although I didn't. So it's good news for you. You will be sent to other places under my banner for stand-up comedy. Your next performance is at Walangkar Auditorium, Colaba. And remember, you were a 'nothing' and remain a 'nothing'."

"Oh, that's great news. Congrats. So it's a beginning of your career. But you aren't looking much happy."

"I am happy. But I am sad too because I have to work with that grumpy man, under his banner."

"I can understand, Sam."

"I am happy because I will receive payment. But I am unhappy because that man never encourages someone's talent."

"Gosh, very true."

Sameer used to go to different places to perform comedy acts. He used to mock at the intense competition in UPSC and SSC, the old lady of his village who smokes beedi, exam pressure on children and the patented dialogue of almost all Indian parents- "Sharma ji's son."

Now our routine became different. Both of us got busy in our own lives. I got indulged in my law assignments, projects and class tests and Sameer got busy in his performances. We started losing our connection. Though we stayed under the same roof, we were living a separate life. We didn't have time to peep into each other's lives. Though Sameer asked me many times to attend his shows, I was very busy in my University's tasks. So he gradually stopped asking me to accompany him. However, we did talk to our parents regularly and told them about our progress. Sameer talked only to his mother. Sameer's and my mother used to send us money through NEFT. I came to know that his father was suffering from high blood pressure, but he didn't seem to be concerned about him. Sameer had, thus, almost forgotten about his father.

One day I was sitting on the study table and was completing my assignment on mercantile law. Suddenly,

Sameer stormed into the room and threw his bag forcefully on the bed. Though we stopped bothering about each other, I became curious to know the matter.

"Sam, what happened? You are looking very angry."

"Harry, there is nothing to say. Damn it. Damn it."

"What happened? I am your brother. Tell me."

Sameer controlled his anger and narrated the incident.

"Today I had a tough fight with Shinde. I could not control my frustration against him and finally busted out."

He started narrating the day's incidents.

"Shinde ji, though 'I' work hard each time to prepare for the shows, 'you' take all the credit. You never acknowledge my hard work and talent."

"Talent! You were a 'nothing' and you are still a 'nothing'…"

"If I am a 'nothing', why do I get standing ovation each time after my performance?"

"Oh you are being proud. All 'nothings' become proud one day and they end up ruining their careers."

"Stop your useless lecture. You are a 'nothing', not I and since two weeks, you are making me do more than one shows in a day. It becomes very painful for me. Moreover, whatever money 'I' earn from my shows, you take away a huge commission out of it and I get only a meagre portion of it".

"You cannot talk to me like that! I am telling you, you cannot survive without me in this huge city. You were a 'nothing' and you will die a 'nothing'. I made you the 'Desi Dude'. The terms and conditions of the firm…"

"Damn your terms and conditions. I am ready to die a 'nothing' rather than working with a useless person and psycho like you. I don't want to work with you anymore."

"Get lost! There are many comedians waiting to work with me. You are not the only one. I will see how you can be a famous comedian without me, 'the Shinde'."

"I left the office and resolved not to return to his office again. I didn't want to even see his dirty face again."

"Gosh Sam! You parted from Shinde. So what will you do next? How will you establish yourself as a comedian?"

"Please don't catapult such harsh questions on me. I am quite confused about what to do now."

I remained silent because I didn't know what to speak next. I resumed thinking about my next week's assignment. But suddenly, Sameer sprang up from the bed in excitement.

"Harry, I have an idea!"

"Oh! Tell me Sam."

"I managed to extract the contact numbers of various organisers of the events. I have the visiting cards of some of them too. So I will contact them and request them to call me for performance."

"Oh that's nice. But will you succeed in this way?"

"I know the future of this step is bleak, but let's try my luck. Harry, you also please talk to your college president and department heads to call me in MNLU."

"Yes I will try. But I can't guarantee you that they will get convinced."

"At least you try buddy."

A phase of hardships again started in Sameer's life. He crazily contacted whomever he knew and requested them to call him for the show. He even reduced his fees to a very low level. Some of them called him in their private functions, but some of them didn't respond as they knew hiring Sameer for a comedy show would mean tarnishing their relationship with Shinde. Whenever I saw him in the room, he looked much stressed and in despair. I felt pity for him. But I found that though he was going through so much stress and hardship, he didn't resort to drastic things such as smoking and drinking. His innocence was persistent in his conduct. That's why a timid and meek guy like me found in him a suitable companion.

I also tried my best to lobby the student and department leaders to hire Sameer for the fests and farewell events. I thought that as I wasn't a good convincer, I will not succeed. However, something else happened. I entered our room and saw him sipping hot tea.

"Sam! I have news for you."

"Oh! First let me finish my tea."

"Keep aside that cup of tea. I have a special thing for you."

"Okay okay. Tell me," he spoke after keeping the cup aside and covering it with a saucer.

"The student leader of the mercantile law department has agreed to call you for the department farewell event. She was impressed by your videos on YouTube and agreed to pay you a reasonable amount."

"Oh thank you sooooo much!" he said while dancing in joy. The stress seemed to fade away from his face and he looked very happy. He hugged me tightly.

"The student leader, Juhi Kashyap, said that she will call you by evening about the dates and other requirements."

"Thank you so much, Harry bhai."

I saw Sameer sitting with his mobile phone since afternoon for the phone call. He didn't even eat lunch. Whenever I asked him to have some, he refused saying that first he will talk to the organiser and then have something. I was praying to God in my mind for an early phone call from Juhi, so that he breaks his fast and eats something.

A phone call came from an unsaved number on his mobile at around 5.30 pm. He picked up the phone in excitement. The mobile signal was breaking in the room, so he went to the terrace to take the call. It was Juhi's call. He talked to her regarding the show's date, timing, venue, etc for almost one hour. I did nothing but gaze at him.

As his conversation was over, he rushed into the room and started screaming with joy.

"Mr. Harish Harry, the Desi Dude is coming to MNLU next week on Wednesday for the farewell party. Juhi ma'am asked me to prepare jokes on the legal system of our country and the life of a law student."

"Oh kudos. Cheers."

I was very happy. We decided to go out to have Pav Bhaji near Akberalli to celebrate the moment.

ELEVEN

The week passed quickly and Wednesday arrived. Sameer had worked very hard for his performance in MNLU. I also helped him a bit regarding the life of a law student and the current situation of the legal system of our country.

Both of us were so excited that we woke up very early. The event was in afternoon. Sameer had some tasks to do, so he left early. I had my breakfast and was selecting my dress for the farewell. Suddenly my phone started ringing. I saw that it was Sameer's mother's call. I picked it up.

"Hello aunty ji. Harish this side."

"Harish beta...," her voice was trembling.

"Yes aunty ji."

"Is Sameer near you?"

Her words sounded intense.

"No actually Sameer went out a few minutes ago for some personal tasks." There was a dreadful silence.

"I have been calling him for a long time but his number is out of reach."

"If there is any message, you may tell me, I will inform him."

"Beta...Sameer's father had been suffering from high blood pressure since a long time. Day before yesterday, he had a severe heart attack. I admitted him to the ICU..."

I gulped. Sameer didn't tell me about the health problem of his father.

"He passed away this morning in the ICU."

She started crying. I remained silent as I didn't know what to say.

"If you meet him, please tell him to talk to me."

"Yes..."

She disconnected the call. I was left perplexed. I could not figure out how to convey this message to Sameer on such an important day of his life. I decided to stay in the room to avoid any confrontation with Sameer. However, my University friends were calling and whatsapping me continuously to come to the venue soon. I tried to convince them that I couldn't come, but they were adamant.

I changed my plan and departed for the university. However, I decided to sit in the last row of the auditorium to avoid eye contact with Sameer. My steps seemed heavy and my mind was impaled on the horns of dilemma. I reached the MNLU auditorium fifteen minutes after the scheduled time for his performance. My friends already got seated in the middle row. The auditorium became very noisy due to delay in the performance. Juhi was standing at the main entrance. She saw me and stopped me hurriedly.

"Hey, buddy. Your friend was reluctant to start the programme without seeing you. Where were you? We have many other performances too!"

"I...," I was about to complete the sentence but she interrupted me.

"We have paucity of time. We have kept a seat at the front row vacant for you. I will inform the Desi Dude that his friend has arrived and he may start the performance."

She rushed to the backstage. I didn't have any option but to sit on the indicated seat. A senior guy came to the stage to make the announcement.

"Sometimes it's better to get a bit late," he spoke in a funny tone. The audience started smiling.

"Now let's fill the atmosphere of the hall with some humour. So we would like to call upon the much awaited performer of the afternoon- 'The Desi Dude'!"

The audience started clapping and hooting. Sameer came to the stage in his usual get up. His eyes were searching for me. But he found me sitting on a corner seat of the first row. He looked happy, but my face had an intense look. My hair was unkempt and my eyes turned red in sorrow.

Sameer started his performance. His tone and the honed way of throwing the words was mesmerising the audience. He was frequently looking at me. I tried to smile but I couldn't. This made him fumble many times. But he covered up his fumbling tactfully. I could guess that he was getting uncanny indication that there was something wrong. My eyes were getting wet as he was speaking.

The cycle continued for around twenty minutes and he was getting annoyed. Suddenly he left the stage through the left wing. The audience and the organisers were amazed. Then he entered the auditorium from one of the gates. The audience were hooting and took out their mobile phones to take his pictures. He dashed to me hurriedly. The organisers could not figure out what was happening.

Sameer came to me and held my wrist tightly and dragged me out of the auditorium. I could hear Juhi shouting behind us, "Hey man, you have to perform for an hour more. You can't go like this. Wait. Stop!" But he avoided her yells and took me out of the auditorium.

"Harry! How is my father?" he asked. I got scared. He knew that there was something wrong with his father.

I remained silent as I couldn't decide how to tell him. In the meantime, I could see some of the members of the organising team were sprinting towards us. I gathered courage and spoke to him.

"He is no more... He passed away in the ICU." I was choking while I was speaking. Sameer turned pale like a stone and he fell on his knees. I gestured to the sprinting members of the organising committee to stop. They stopped and guessed that there was something wrong. I whispered the entire incident in brief in the ears of one of them. Fortunately he felt sympathetic for him and asked the members to retreat. I took him to the water cooler and asked him to drink some water and splash water on his face. Then I kept my arm on his shoulder and ushered him to our room.

When we crossed the auditorium, I heard someone announcing in the microphone, "Guys, the Desi Dude had to leave due to some unavoidable family issues. We invite the members of the Dance society to perform, so that the next participants can get ready."

As we reached our room, I asked him to lie on the bed. I brought a glass of water for him, which he drank slowly. I was amazed to see that he was lamenting for his father, whom he disliked and who broke all his relations with his son. After getting pacified a bit, he pulled out his mobile phone from his pocket. We found that it was in Airplane mode. That's why his mother couldn't contact him.

Sameer went to the terrace to call his mother. Both talked for a long time and tears were rolling out of his eyes while he was talking. I also felt very sad for him as it was a huge setback for him at such a crucial stage of his career.

After about an hour, he entered the room and sat on the bed without uttering a word. I sat beside him. He lifted his head and looked at me.

"Harish, I know why you are shocked to see me lamenting for my father."

"Oh actually...," I was completing the sentence but he interrupted.

"No need to give any diplomatic answer. I am recalling the days when I was a small kid and my father used to make me sit around his neck and showed me the village fair. He used to take me to a Golgappa stall. He used to put the Golgappas gently into my small mouth."

I remained silent. I again didn't know what to say.

"Though he used to scold me each time for poor grades and carelessness, I never back-answered him because I did love him. He scolded me not only for getting a good job in a good company but also because of his desire to see me well-established in life."

I gathered some courage and tried to speak something.

"So bro, what about the last rites of uncle ji?"

"Harry, my mother has booked my flight tickets through an agent and has sent it to me through e-mail. The flight is today at midnight. I will return after two weeks."

"May his soul rest in peace," these were the only words I could speak.

I helped Sameer to pack his bag. After having dinner, we booked a cab to drop us to the airport. It arrived at our location on time. We reached the airport half an hour before the closure of the baggage check-in. He took the boarding pass, bid me goodbye and entered the waiting lounge. I came out of the airport and hired a taxi to drop me to the room.

Next day, I was scared of going to the university. I thought that the organisers might give me a scornful look and the students might shower harsh questions on me. Then I gathered some strength and went to the University. My classmates were staring at me. My close friends were asking me the reason behind the entire episode and I told the entire incident only to them. I tried to ignore my other classmates.

My friends and I went to the canteen, where I met Juhi. She was wearing large spectacles, which made her eyes look cocky and she had a frown on her face. I felt embarrassed in front of her.

"Juhi didi, I am extremely sorry. Everything happened all of a sudden. I...," as I was completing my sentence, she interrupted me.

"Oh no issues. Everything was sorted out properly. It can happen to anyone. The audience enjoyed whatever he did yesterday."

My face lit up after hearing the compassionate words of Juhi.

"And Harish, the best part is that he called me a few hours ago and said that he won't take any money from us. I insisted him to take his remuneration, considering the mishap that occurred in his family, but he was adamant to take anything."

I was again surprised to find that benevolence is still alive in this world after talking to Juhi. Her appearance was completely different from her heart.

It was my final year of LLB in MNLU and I was surrounded by so many assignments and project works. So, I didn't call Sameer for two weeks for two reasons, firstly the two weeks had the deadlines for the completion of the tasks and secondly, I didn't want to disturb him during the last rites of his father. However, I sent a whatsapp message to him saying, "May the Almighty give you strength to bear the great loss."

Sameer returned to Mumbai after two weeks in Bombay Mail from New Delhi. I went to the railway station to see him. He stepped out of the train with his luggage. He had small hairs, as he had to shave off his hairs for the last rites. But he looked jolly. As I said earlier, he was able to manipulate his emotions quickly.

"Harry. How did you spend two weeks without me?" he grinned while speaking.

"Ya, so so," I answered diplomatically.

"I have a complaint that you didn't call me when I was in Delhi. Is there something fishy bro?"

"No actually I didn't want to disturb you during the last rites," I said while hiding the first reason from him, "By the way, how was your journey?"

"It was a bit hectic. You may imagine the journey in a mail train in this hot summer. Will you do all the talking here only or save some of them for the room?"

I didn't answer anything. I took one of his bag and we headed towards the taxi stand. We boarded a taxi and started our conversation when it was midway.

"So, what about aunty ji?"

"Oh mom," he took a deep breath, "though she received the provident fund and gratuity amount of my father, a large portion of it went towards the repayment of the debt. My father didn't have any other investments and he couldn't save much."

"So how will she run the household?"

"My mother talked to a day-care centre for a job of a full time caretaker. She also got a part time job at a beauty parlour. As she couldn't complete her education, she got only this type of job. But I told her that I will try to send her some money each month."

"So now, more hardship."

"But I have complete faith on my comedy. Otherwise, there are so many vegetable markets in this city. I will sit in one of them with a cart," he said half jokingly.

We were having a long conversation and the taxi was moving along the sea shore. The sun was shining very brightly that day. There was scorching heat, but it did not stop the pedlars, dabbawalas and vegetable sellers from their work. Our conversation lessened the journey and we couldn't figure out how we reached the room so quickly.

TWELVE

Sameer always tried to cover up his dilemma and anxiety with his comedy, but I could see that he was pushed into more hardship. He went out of the room early in the morning and returned late at night. He went for auditions for side roles in different movies. But he got rejected each time. He also went for auditions for TV commercials, but he didn't succeed. Though he claimed that everything was all right, his face reflected his despair.

Finally, he got a job of a part time worker at a movie theatre. He worked from morning to evening there. He went for auditions in between. The money he earned got consumed for the room rent, his mother's daily provisions and our daily provisions. His mother also helped him a bit by sending money.

As his earnings increased a bit, he joined a nearby gym. He found that a nice body is required to impress the masses. So we hardly saw each other in the room.

So four months elapsed. Sameer's body was changing from thin to a fleshy and muscular one. He started looking like a model.

One day, we were together in our room. He was looking a bit ecstatic. I thought that there was good news.

"Hey Desi Dude! Looking jolly today. Any news?"

"Harry! I just got a call from the G.Morning Coffee. It is a foreign brand of coffee which is launching its product in our country by organising an event to showcase the talent of stand-up comedians, musical bands and freestyle dancers."

"Wow that's great news!"

"However there is a small problem."

"What problem?"

"The caller told me that he saw my video on YouTube. He was impressed, but he wants me to change my style of comedy."

"Sam, can you be more specific?"

"The guy told me that since the coffee is exotic in nature, I have to speak in English!" Sameer said in amusement.

"English!"

"Yes. I used to mug up the English guide before the English exams and somehow managed to pass them."

"Well, if you require, I will help you."

"Oh thanks bro. You saved me," Sameer said after taking a sigh of relief.

"You tell me your jokes in Hindi, I will translate them in English."

"Oh nice, Harry."

It was a golden opportunity for him and he decided to utilise it. He told me the jokes and short funny poems in Hindi and I gave him the English translations. I also helped him to speak without fumbling. He also worked very hard to make his speech fluent as well as humorous.

On November 22, he went to the studio for the programme. He wore a nice sweatshirt and jeans. He wore a small brown hat, which he purchased last week. He insisted me a lot to accompany him, but I had to prepare for the final exam. But I knew that the coffee company would upload the video on YouTube, where I could see his performance.

When he returned from the event at 1 am, I was awake.

"Hey Sam, how was it?"

"Very nice! I was surprised that I could change my genre. The audience and the organisers appreciated my performance. They also gave me an offer to endorse their brand in their commercial."

"What did you tell them?"

"Harry, it's not so easy. I told them that I will decide and inform them shortly. But why are you still awake bro?"

"Exams..."

"Okay. Carry on."

A couple of days later, I saw that the coffee company uploaded the video on YouTube. Sameer was looking amazing in the video. His tone was completely changed. It seemed that his mother tongue was English! The company uploaded the video with the caption, "Desi Guy Goes Videsi." The video got 5K likes within one day.

I went to the university. I saw that a group of girls dashed towards me.

"Hey dude. I heard that the 'Desi Dude' stays with you. Is it true?"

"Ya, yes."

"We are his huge fan after watching yesterday's video. He is that guy who came in the farewell function, right."

"Yeah."

"I am impressed by his accent, so masculine," a girl present in the group whispered among them.

I guessed instantly that his video had gone viral on Whatsapp, Instagram and Snapchat too. Similarly many juniors and seniors came to me and asked the same thing. I was feeling like a celebrity.

That day, Sameer was present in the room for the entire day. I came to the room and sat besides him.

"Sam, do you know your performance at the G. Morning Coffee Studio got viral on Facebook, Whatsapp and Snapchat."

"Oh wow. I saw today morning that the video has got 5K views on YouTube."

"Sam, today many students came to me and asked about you. I was feeling like a celebrity."

"Oh nice. Today I got a call from an employee of the G. Morning Coffee for my decision about the commercial. And guess what, I agreed."

"Wonderful, man!"

Sameer endorsed the coffee brand on newspapers and magazines. He also got offers for endorsing local products of Mumbai on local newspapers, magazines and TV channels. The wheels of his career had again started revolving.

THIRTEEN

"Hello mom."

I got a call from mom in the afternoon. "Hello Hari beta. How are you?"

"Fine, mom."

"Beta, can you come out of your room for a while. I need to talk to you."

I was anxious about what mother would tell me. Did I commit any mistake? Was there anything wrong at my home in Delhi? I came out of the room to the terrace to listen to my mom.

"Mom, I am at the terrace."

"What's your partner Sameer doing right now?"

"He is sleeping."

"Sleeping! Its 1 pm!"

"Actually yesterday he returned at 3 am. He had gone for some performance at the outskirts of Mumbai."

"Hari, as you know, it is a very crucial stage of your life. Success requires discipline and punctuality. Without these qualities, you won't be able to achieve your goals."

"Yes mom," I rejoiced after listening to the motivational words from my mom.

"But if you stay with Sameer, you will definitely lose these qualities. So I would advise you either change your PG or ask your friend to find a PG for himself. Don't stay with him anymore."

My happiness immediately turned into despair.

"But mom, he is undergoing through a pathetic phase of his life. His father passed away and he has broken his ties with Shinde. He requires a companion. I can't leave him!"

"Beta, we have never pressurised you for anything in your life and we will never. But it's your choice whether you want to succeed in your life or just simply ruin it!"

"Mom, but..."

"It's your choice, man. Now you are a grown up guy and we cannot coax you to do anything. But as a mother, I can only advise you for your betterment."

She disconnected the call. I was completely taken aback. I was baffled about whose side to be taken- mom's side or Sameer's side.

Sameer woke up at 3 pm. I was sitting with an assignment.

"Harry, you are still doing your assignment."

"Yes, we have to submit it tomorrow itself."

I was feeling gloomy as I saw his face. I was unable to ask him to leave or I leave myself.

"Harry dude, yesterday it was a very tiring performance. The venue was far too."

"Yes bro, I can understand." I tried not to express my grief to him. I didn't have the courage to talk to him.

Next day Sameer returned home at night. I was reading the theory of mercantile law. As I saw him, I gathered courage to tell him the issue.

"Sam, actually... basically... I want to tell you something."

"That you are going to become a father! Ha ha," he said frivolously.

"Sam, you are so..."

"Mean, right. He he."

"Now jokes apart, I want to admit something very serious."

"Shukla, even I want to tell you something. It is also very serious."

"No first I will say," I insisted.

"No I will say. I always listen to you first. But today, you will listen to me," he sounded adamant.

"Okay, you say first."

"Shukla, now I am going to have a very rigorous schedule. When I will return from tomorrow is very uncertain. Your final exams are approaching and my schedule may hamper your study environment," he was repeating my own words. "So Shukla, I have seen a PG at Nariman Point for myself and I will shift there shortly. I don't want to hinder your studies."

"But Sam..."

"I know you also wanted this for a long time. By the way, whenever I see your thick and heavy books on mer... mer..."

I was shocked to find out that he knew what I wanted.

"Mercantile laws."

"Yes, mercantile laws, I get inferiority complex. They just frighten me a lot."

"But such a drastic decision. Please reconsider your decision. We can stay here together."

"Don't act smart. I have already talked to my new landlord. But if you want to do something for me, do come and meet me frequently, I will be happy."

"Okay..." I said meekly.

Two days later, a taxi was standing at the doorstep of the PG. Both of us were putting Sameer's luggage into the taxi. I was both happy and upset. I thought he might also have the same feelings. When we completed putting the luggage, we both looked at each other with eyes full of sorrow.

"Sam, please return here after my exams. We have spent five years together."

"Shukla, our careers got bifurcated long ago. Now, it's time to bifurcate our lives. As we move on from this diversion, it will be very difficult for us to return back to this same point. It's time for both of us to get established in our lives. But do stay connected with me. I don't want to bifurcate our friendship."

I remained silent. I tried to say something.

"Bro, I can at least say goodbye?"

He didn't utter a word and hugged me. Both of us stopped our tears from rolling as we were standing in a public place. Then he sat in the taxi and departed for his new PG. I was looking at it till it got disappeared in the horizon.

I returned to the room. The beautiful moments that we spent together were flashing in my mind- the scooty rides, night outs, accompanying him to the comedy shows, irritating him with the incidents at MNLU, etc. I resolved that I will go to meet him regularly once my final exams got over.

I called my mom to give her the news.

"Hello mom."

"Hello beta. What's up?"

"Mom, Sameer has shifted to a new rented flat."

"Thank God, you have saved your career. Wow."

"So mom, now you are happy?"

Suddenly her tone got changed. She got vexed after hearing my last statement.

"Listen Hari, I told you to part from him for your betterment. I am not a foe of your friendship with that comedian. I want to see you getting successful in your career, which can happen only if you stay away from him. If you want, go and stay with him again and return to Delhi with a ruined career."

I stayed quiet.

"Don't worry beta. When your final exams will be over, both of you can again stay together."

I couldn't say anything to her.

"Okay mom," I said in a hush voice.

"Love you beta. Goodbye."

She disconnected the call.

A few days after parting with Sameer, I was studying for the final exams, which were commencing the next week. My phone started ringing. It was an unknown number. I picked it up.

"Hello."

"Hello. Is it Harish Shukla's number?"

"Yes, I am Harish Shukla."

"Hi Harish, this is Himanshu this side."

"Oh Himanshu, after so many years. How are you, dude?"

"I am fine bro. How are you?"

"Fine. Himanshu, I called you many times after coming to Mumbai, but your number remained out of reach."

"Yes actually all my contacts of my old mobile phone got deleted and I discontinued my old SIM card long ago. I found your number in an old notebook, so I decided to call you."

"It's nice to talk to you after such a long time. What are you doing these days?"

"Harish, I came to Mumbai last month for an internship at a media house. The internship is a part of my BJMC course at Bharatiya Vidyapeeth. You are doing LLB from MNLU, right."

"Yes bro. This is my final year here."

"Do you have any information about Sameer, our comedian? I completely lost all contact with him after the declaration of the Board results."

"Oh he also came to Mumbai with me to pursue his career in comedy."

I narrated the entire story to him about Sameer in Mumbai. Himanshu seemed fascinated by his story.

"Oh now I got it, Harish."

"What?"

"I saw a billboard which had an advertisement in which a muscular guy was standing with a packet of flour in his hand. The guy looked like Sameer. So my motive of calling you was also to confirm whether he was Sameer or not."

"Yes, it can be Sameer. After performing for G. Morning Coffee, he was getting offers to endorse local products. He has worked in many small advertisements."

"Wow, so our friend is becoming a celebrity. Cool."

"Yes."

"So Harish, it was really nice to talk to you. Now I have to leave for my office. I will talk to you later. Goodbye."

"Bye Himanshu, good day."

Even I also started finding advertisements with Sameer's image in the local newspapers and magazines. Some of my friends told me that they saw him in the commercials shown in Marathi TV channels. So Sameer's career was flourishing.

FOURTEEN

"Tell us something about yourself, Mr. Harish Shukla."

The placement season started at MNLU. I gave interview for jobs in different companies for the post of legal advisor. The panellist of one of the interview asked me the question.

"I see myself as a dynamic and hardworking person..."

I answered almost all the questions of the interviews. It was a very eventful day of my life. I was waiting for the placement results, which would be declared by the university after a month. I came back to my room and immediately called my dad.

"Hello dad."

"Hi Hari beta, how were your interviews?" dad asked.

"Well... nice dad."

"Did you answer the questions confidently?"

"Yes dad."

"I know you are a smart person and you will be able to crack the interview of a reputed company," dad said in an encouraging tone.

"Dad, let's hope for the best."

"Have you eaten something, my child?"

"Not yet, dad."

"Immediately eat something, Hari beta. It was a very eventful day and you might be tired. I will call you later. Bye"

"Bye dad."

I plugged in the charger of the phone and went to the kitchen to have something. I found some cornflakes and there was milk in the refrigerator. As I was eating cornflakes with milk, my phone started ringing. It was Sameer's call.

"Hi Harry."

"Oh hi Sam. How are you bro?"

"Fine, the new place is nice. However, the landlady is a bit grumpy and money hungry."

"Where are you now, bro?"

"I am returning from the gym. Well, how was your interview?"

"Oh you remembered that today I had interviews!"

"Harry, do you think I am Ghajini? Ha ha."

"No no. Ha ha..."

"I am glad that my schedule is becoming busier. I am getting many contracts from different organisers and firms."

"That's very nice, Desi Dude."

"Harry bro, I have to meet someone today, some organiser. I will talk to you later. Wish you best of luck for your placement. Goodbye."

"Okay bye dude."

He disconnected the call. I was glad that he remembered my placement date in spite of a busy schedule and so many things to remember.

I gave the final exams. The exams spanned for one and a half month. There were so many subjects in the final semester. Now I was free and wanted to relax. I called Sameer just after giving the last exam.

"Hello Sam."

"Hi Shukla, how are you."

"Fine Desi Dude. Today my exams got over. So when shall I come to meet you?"

"Oh let me think..."

"So do I need to talk to your secretary for appointment?" I said jokingly.

"No I haven't kept any secretary till now. You can come to my room tomorrow after 2 pm."

"Can you tell me the address of your PG?"

"Dude, I will whatsapp you my location."

"Sameer I want to tell you..."

"Harry I am in the gym right now. I will listen to you tomorrow at my PG and remember, if you don't find me in the room, just wait for me there."

"Okay you carry on."

He disconnected the call. I found that he had already became a mini celebrity, with so much work and time constraint.

Next day I prepared his favourite *lithi chokha* and packed it in a tiffin box. Sameer had whatsapped me his room's location the previous night. I took a taxi to go to his new residence. I reached the destination at 2.15 pm. I rang the doorbell of the ground floor. An old lady came out with a walking stick.

"Who are you, young boy? Have you come here for a room on rent?"

"I am Harish Shukla. I have come here to meet my friend Sam, no Sameer Mishra."

"Oh Sameer, that Delhi guy. He stays on the third floor."

"Thank you, ma'am."

"And tell your friend to pay me the rent without any delay. I find Delhi people completely unreliable."

She closed the door. I wanted to break her stereotype about Delhiites, but I ignored her.

I went straight through a tapestry, then climbed the stairs and rang the doorbell of his room. I found that the door was unlocked. I entered the room. It was a single room with a single bed and an attached bathroom and a kitchen. There was a small window, but a building was just a few centimetres away from it. So, no one could see anything from it.

Sameer had the habit of keeping his room very untidy. I was not finding any place on the floor to stand. The entire floor was filled with chips wrappers, unwashed clothes, socks, magazines, empty cans of energy drinks, etc. The room was stinky too. Somehow I made way through the stuff lying on the floor and sat on the bed, after removing more stuff lying on the bed.

I was about to call Sameer but I recalled that he told me to wait if I didn't find him in his room. So I looked at the walls of the room. The left wall was full of sticky notes on which various addresses, contact numbers, important dates, etc. were written. On the right wall, there were newspaper and magazines cut outs with his photograph. The cut outs mostly had advertisements of various local products. As my vision went towards the tubelight, I saw a small portrait of his father with a garland on it. I was shocked to see that he respected the person, who once disowned him.

Around twenty minutes had passed and nobody came to the room. I kept waiting. I looked down and I was shocked. The corner of the room had dumbbells of different weights and bottles of different protein supplements required for workout.

Suddenly the door opened. I looked at it and saw Sameer entering. I noticed that he had turned more muscular than before. Muscles were protruding from different parts of his body. His face was glowing and he had a new hairstyle. He was looking amazing in his new muscular body.

"Oh Shukla, you have come."

We hugged each other as we met after such a long time.

"Sam, I have been waiting for you since a very long time."

"Bro, actually I had to go to meet an advertising firm for a new assignment. Yesterday I wasn't sure about its date, so I asked you to wait for me if you don't find me."

"And what about the room? It is so dirty."

"Bro, yesterday I returned here very late- at around 3 am. I couldn't pick up the stuff. I know you are a huge cleanliness-lover, but work pressure, you can understand."

"Mr. Desi Dude, I have found that you have wasted too much money on the supplements."

"Yes Shukla, some advertisers pressurised me to have a nice physique for their ads. Otherwise, they would hire someone else. Now, how could I have produced a muscular physique in such a short time?"

"And…"

"Hey bro, have you come here to meet me or for showering so many complaints and questions on me?"

I stopped my interrogation. I was so excited that I completely forgot what I was doing.

"Okay, Desi Dude. I have cooked your favourite *lithi chokha* for you."

"Oh thank you so much bro. Shukla, let's have it together. I am bringing plates and bowl."

"Okay, but first let's both of us clean up the room. The condition of the room is not suitable for eating anything."

"Okay bro, as you wish."

Both of us removed the stuff from the floor and the bed and disposed off the garbage. Then Sameer warmed up the food in his kitchen and brought plates. I unfolded an old newspaper and laid it on the bed to have the food. Sameer served the *lithi chokha*. We again started chatting while eating.

"Sam, when did you change your hairstyle?"

"Last week bro, from Javed Habib. Isn't it nice?"

"It's spectacular."

"Yesterday you were saying that you wanted to tell me something wonderful."

"Oh yes. A week before my exams, Himanshu called me."

"Himanshu, our friend at The Success House in Delhi."

"Yes."

"What's that brat doing these days?"

"He is in the final year of Journalism and Mass Communication at Bharatiya Vidyapeeth, Pune. He is doing an internship in Mumbai in one of the media houses."

"Okay. Why hasn't that character called me till now?"

"He said that he had changed his mobile and all contacts of his earlier mobile got deleted."

"So Desi Dude. You are slowly becoming a huge celebrity. So will you continue with the comedy shows and advertisements or do something else?"

"Shukla, I love doing comedy shows. But I want to bring versatility in my life. That's why I am working a lot on my physique and looks."

"Oh I see."

"Oh yes Shukla, I forgot to tell you. I gave the audition for Splitsvilla. Have you heard about it?"

"Yes I know. It is aired on MTV. It is a famous stunt based youth programme."

"Yes true. Now let's see if I get selected for it or not."

We finished the mini lunch. I wished to stay for some more time with him, but I had to go to MNLU for filling a form.

"Shukla, it was very nice to meet you after such a long time. Keep coming here to meet me."

"Yes sure, bro. Oh I remember, your landlady has asked me to tell you to pay your rent without any delay," I said jokingly.

"Oh she is just Shinde's counterpart. She starts asking for the rent very early. Though I had to pay her a hefty security deposit, she keeps making fuss for the rent."

"Her words indicated that she dislikes Delhiites."

Sameer nodded.

"So Desi Dude, I will meet you soon."

"Yes."

We hugged each other and I departed for MNLU. It was dusk and I was travelling in an auto-rickshaw. The auto went through the marine drive road. I was continuously looking at the sea and recalling my meeting with Sameer.

FIFTEEN

"Hello Mom, how are you?" I called my mom in excitement. The placement results were declared. I went to the University to see the notice board, where the names of the selected candidates and the employer's name were written.

"Nice Hari beta."

"Nice Mom. Mom there is good news."

"What news beta?"

"Mom, you know I gave interviews for placement in MNLU. I have received a job offer from M.G. Developers Ltd. for the post of Assistant Legal Advisor. The company is in Bangalore. The package is ten lakhs per annum, including basic pay and other perks."

"Oh congratulations my child. Well done. Your father will be very happy."

My mother rushed to dad and told her the news. He took the mobile phone from her.

"Hari we are proud of you. I will inform all our relatives and friends. Nobody in our family has received such high figured salary in his entire lifetime. Love you, my child."

"I love you dad."

"So beta, when is your joining date?"

"It is in September. So I still have four months gap. I have already booked my rail tickets to Bangalore. The company will provide me accommodation."

"Nice. We are very happy, dear."

"Thanks dad, bye."

I disconnected the phone. My other friends at MNLU also got placed in well-known firms. I decided to call Sameer to tell him the news. I dialled his number.

"Hello Harry."

"Hi Sam, I have some good news."

"I also have good news, Harry. I was about to call."

"First I will tell Sam."

"Okay, tell me."

"Sam, I have got a job for the post of legal advisor at a company located in Bangalore."

"Wow. So your dream has come true."

"Yes. I have to join in September. Till then I am free. Now tell me your news."

"Yesterday I got a call from the Splitsvilla team. They told me that I am selected for the show! Now I will come on TV!"

"Oh that's great. So when will you leave?"

"I will leave next week for the show. So we will not be able to meet each other for a long time."

"I will stay connected with you through mobile phone. We will surely meet soon."

"Yes bro. So, best of luck. Goodbye, Harry."

"Best of luck to you too. Goodbye."

He disconnected the phone. Next week I went to meet him

near Akberalli, a day before his departure for the Splitsvilla journey.

"So Sam, people will see you on a national television channel. Aren't you excited?"

"Yes Shukla, I am highly excited."

"So Sameer, we may not be able to meet again as I will leave for Bangalore before you return from the show."

Sameer nodded in gloom.

"At least stay connected with me through Facebook, Whatsapp and Insta."

"Yes definitely." I saw a Cafe Coffee Day outlet near Akberalli. "Let's have coffee at CCD."

"Okay."

Both of us went to the CCD outlet. We sat on one of the red coloured chairs. I ordered a cup of regular coffee and he ordered a sugar-free regular coffee.

"So Harry, this can be our last meeting too. I have noticed that when even two best friends enter into new lives, they get disconnected."

"I will ensure that we stay connected. I will try to come to Mumbai during the leaves. You also try to come to Bangalore."

"Yes sure. Harry,"

In the meantime our coffees were served. We sipped it while chatting further.

When we were leaving the CCD, Sameer looked at me.

"Harry, I have to go to my room for packing. I wish you a good luck for your job."

"I also wish you a good luck. Just win the show and become a huge celebrity."

Both of us hugged each other and left for our rooms. I was feeling bad that I may not see Sam again.

SIXTEEN

"Harry, can you come to meet me at my room right now?" It was 10 pm at night. It had been almost two weeks since Sameer left for the show. I was shocked to find that he was calling me to his room. He sounded very desperate.

"But it's too late."

"Please for God's sake, come to meet me."

"Okay I am coming," I got frightened.

I disconnected the call. I removed the earphones and called an Uber cab.

I reached his room at around 10.30 pm.

I quietly entered his room. I saw him sitting with his palm on his face. Tears were rolling out of his eyes. I sat beside him.

"Hey Desi Dude..."

"Don't call me with that name bro," he interrupted me and spoke angrily.

"Ok Sam, I heard about a controversy about you and a Delhi girl at Splitsvilla. It is getting viral on Whatsapp and Facebook."

"Yes I want to tell you about that only."

"As I went for the Splitsvilla journey, a girl named Shalini Verma, who was a Delhiite was made my partner. We had performed many tasks together and won them. Both of us were rapidly moving towards victory. Gradually both of us fell in love with each other. She often came to me and I started flirting with her. I proposed her after one of the tasks and she accepted my proposal.

One day she asked me to come to her room. I went there. She was wearing a very attractive dress. She started kissing me and seducing me. I thought that she was genuinely willing to make love with me. Both of us got intimate and enjoyed the moment. However the next day, I found that someone had spread the video of our intimate moment. Shalini suddenly got angry in front of the host and she blamed me for secretly capturing the video and making it viral to defame her and get publicity. I tried to convince everyone that I was innocent, but nobody paid heed to my words and the hosts evicted me from the show."

Now the media is broadcasting dreadful headlines like 'Desi Dude, a Cruel Dude', 'Desi Dude, a shameless male chauvinist', etc. The video is also getting viral. I am unable to move out of the room, I cannot even go to the gym.

Shukla, trust me, I loved Shalini from the bottom of my heart. I can't do such a ruthless thing."

He started weeping after telling his story. I put my hand on his head to console him.

"Don't cry Sam. I trust you. You can't do such an awful thing."

"What can I do now? My Splitsvilla journey as well as comedy career have got ruined. Now I am just a 'nothing'. I am sad for two things, one is that I have lost my career and second is that Shalini was my first love. I had fully committed myself to her. She cheated me so badly."

"Have faith in God, there will surely be a way to prove your innocence."

"But I don't have any evidence."

"Let me think of a way."

"Harry, do you remember that at CCD, we considered that meeting as our last meeting for a long time. I didn't expect that I would meet you again so shortly and in such an awful situation..." he broke down after saying this.

Sameer was sitting on the bed and I was probing along the bed to find out a way using my knowledge of LLB.

"Hey do you have any idea about the character of Shalini?"

"She is a bitch. She got direct entry into the show as her father was the Managing Director of the company that sponsored the programme. She didn't give any auditions."

"Hey Sam, let's talk to Himanshu. He is in the media line. He can give us some advice. Shall I call him?"

"Okay. Do the needful."

I took out my mobile phone from the pocket and called Himanshu.

"Hi Himanshu!"

"Hello Harish bro."

"Sorry to call you so late at night, but there is a serious issue with Sameer."

"Are you talking about the Shalini Verma controversy?"

"Yes yes."

"What a coincidence! I got an assignment to gather information about this case for the Page 3."

"Oh very nice! So can you please come to Sameer's PG now? We wanted to discuss the matter together. I will send you the location."

"Tonight I have to complete an assignment. I will definitely come tomorrow early in the morning."

"Okay but do come."

"Okay bye."

He disconnected the call. I whatsapped him the location of Sameer's PG. Then I turned to him.

"I have talked to Himanshu. He has promised that he will come early in the morning."

Sameer sat with his head bowed down.

"Bro, have you eaten anything?"

"No," he said in a very low voice.

I went into his kitchen without asking him whether he wanted to eat anything or not. I opened the door of his refrigerator and found an egg and a loaf of bread. I made bread toast and omelette on the gas stove. Luckily, gas was left in his LPG cylinder.

I brought the mini dinner for him.

"Have it bro. You are looking very weak."

"I don't want to eat anything."

"Eat it without uttering a word. Himanshu and I will ensure that you get justice."

He ate the dinner. He asked me to stay in his room overnight. I was making the agenda, while Sameer was sitting in grief.

At 5 am, someone knocked at the door. I knew it was Himanshu. I opened the door to receive him.

"Hey Harry. Where's Sameer?"

"He is sitting right there."

Himanshu went straight to Sameer.

"Hi Sameer. Seeing you after so many years."

"Hi bro. I never expected that I will meet you again in such an awful situation."

"Don't worry, things will be in our hands soon," Himanshu said.

"Himanshu, you said that you were working on this issue. What have you discovered till now?" I asked him.

"All news channels are showing Sameer as the villain. But I do believe that he is not. However due to lack of evidence and as our media house is new, we have to be a sheep of the herd. We have to show the same thing."

"But have some mercy on our dear friend. Let's find the 'janamkundli' of Shalini Verma. It will give a new angle to the story and it will also give publicity to your media house," I told him boldly.

"But how can I do that?" he asked meekly.

"Let's meet Shalini's close friends, relatives and employees of her father's company. We will bring her true colours out in the media. We can also do sting operations if required. If other media houses are showing Sameer as the villain, we can show Shalini as the villain."

"Nice idea Harry. But you need to work swiftly for this. Otherwise, the Splitsvilla season will end," Sameer said by actively participating in the discussion.

"Himanshu, this operation can also enable you to get a nice appraisal. Remember; don't let anyone know that Sameer is our friend. You have to work as a third person. I will help you."

"Thanks Harry. I will work hard to save the reputation and fame of our dear friend," Himanshu said.

"Thank you my friends," Sameer said.

"Mention not. But we need to start from today itself," I said boldly.

Himanshu patted Sameer's shoulder and he left for his expedition. In the meantime, I plotted other parameters through which we could trap Shalini Verma.

SEVENTEEN

"Hey guys, I have found the entire history of that witch," Himanshu said.

Three of us met again at Sameer's PG two days after our first meeting.

"Oh nice! Please share with us," I said in an excited tone.

"I secretly met many classmates and friends of Shalini. I came to know that Shalini has been a spoilt girl since her teenage. She started smoking and consuming cocaine and cannabis since ninth standard. She used to go to pubs and lounges frequently to have beer. She had many boyfriends since her teenage. Her father is the Managing Director of a Mumbai-based company."

"Oh my God," I said in amazement.

"I probed many local newspapers and found that many cases have been registered against her. She was once caught dealing with drugs at a famous lounge in Mumbai. Many cases of drinking and driving are already registered against her."

Himanshu took a pause. We were eager to listen more about her.

"She is doing modelling."

"So Sam, see what type of a girl you loved," I said. Sameer hid his face with his palm.

"Himanshu, I think she did all this to get huge cash reward from any of the other male contestants whose competitor was Sameeer," I said in a detective's accent. "And Himanshu, thanks for your wonderful report on Shalini Verma."

"Mention not."

"I have checked the Whatsapp conversation between Shalini and Sameer. Sameer only praised her beauty and her skills to perform the tasks. He wrote motivational things, funny shayaris and jokes to her. It was Shalini who wrote seductive things since the beginning of the chats. Her words showed that she was trying to attract Sameer towards her. However Sameer always tried to divert the things. Shalini's call to Sameer to ask him to come to her room was a part of her dirty plot," I said.

"Oh I see," Himanshu said.

"See the last message from Shalini. *She wrote, 'I know I was the one who hid a secret camera in my room. Just quietly fuck off from the show without making any fuss. Otherwise I will put a legal case on you, which will take away your remaining honour and freedom. You don't know me and my father.'*"

"Harry and Himanshu, there is an impetus for your plan," Sameer said.

"What impetus?" Himanshu and I said in unison.

"I made a friend, who is a part of the production crew of Splitsvilla. He is also from Kanpur. I called and asked him to send me the CCTV footage of the night when everything happened. The CCTV camera was installed near her room. He e-mailed me the footage. See, here it is," Sameer said.

He took out his mobile phone and played the video. The footage showed that Shalini installed a camera in a flower vase before Sameer entered her room. She installed it to capture the intimate moments.

"Oh the video will make us the winner of the game," I said in amusement.

After seeing the video, three of us made an action plan.

"So friends, proceed as we have decided," Sameer said.

Three of us went straight to the studio of the media house. Himanshu took permission from his seniors to broadcast his findings. His seniors found our idea to provide the controversy a new angle wonderful. They gave permission to him to go ahead with the plan.

Sameer at first submitted the report to the news reporter. She started reading about the character and history of Shalini Verma live on the news channel. Though it was a new media house, the report got huge number of views instantly.

Then in one of the rooms of the studio, Sameer sat in front of a white background. His face had an intense look. A camera was kept in front of him to capture the video. The camera man called "Three, two, and one, start."

"Hi, I am Sameer Mishra, the Desi Dude. I have been shown as a villain in most of the TV channels. I am honestly speaking, I never intended to capture and leak the intimate scenes between me and Shalini. I have evidence to show that I am not guilty."

He took out his mobile phone and opened up the chat with Shalini. The camera zoomed in on the chat.

"See viewers the chats, especially the last message from her. I know most you may think that the chats are fake. I have another evidence to prove my innocence. See the video."

He played the CCTV footage on his mobile phone.

"I hope the video is enough to prove my innocence. I also hope that you must have heard by now about the true character of Shalini Verma. I have full faith that the organisers of Splitsvilla will do the needful."

The news channel circulated the video on the social networking sites, which became viral in a few hours. It started getting various calls from the viewers who were Desi Dude's fans who were supporting him. Some of the fans launched an online signature campaign to put pressure on the organisers of Splitsvilla to retake Sameer in their show and take strict action against Shalini Verma. The reporters were continuously showing the CCTV footage, whatsapp chats and the history of Shalini. The TRP of the news channel rose rapidly that day.

Sameer sent the entire package of video, chats and history. The news channel got threats from Shalini's father, but the management of the channel didn't stop the reporting as they didn't want to lose the growth in their TRP. The episode continued for two days. The online campaign of Desi Dude's fans got twenty-seven likes in two days. We were surprised to find that Sameer had so many fans.

EIGHTEEN

"Guys, we have finally won the battle," Sameer exclaimed in joy. Three of us were on a conference call. Sameer had some great news to share.

"The organisers of Splitsvilla called me. They are giving me a wild card entry in the semi- finals! They apologised for evicting me."

"Wow bro! Congrats!" Himanshu and I spoke together.

"The best part is that the show evicted Shalini. They recognised my innocence."

"Finally our endeavour to put pressure on the organisers of the show became fruitful," I said.

"Yes. I also came to know something from my secret sources," Sameer said.

"What bro?" Himanshu said.

"A contestant named Harry Nanda bribed Shalini to plot against me. I was the biggest obstacle in his path. The show is evicting him too. Shalini's father's company withdrew from sponsoring the show, but it found new sponsors quickly. I also came to know that long ago, when I gave audition to Shinde and only five guys, including me were selected, Harry Nanda also gave the audition there along with me. But he couldn't qualify the audition and he got jealous of me since that time. He made the plot with Shalini to destroy my career out of his jealousy."

"Oh I see," I said.

"Who's this Shinde? What audition are you talking about?"

"Oh Himanshu, it's a very long story. I will tell you someday later," Sameer said.

"So when will you go to the villa again?" I asked

"Tomorrow."

"What!" I said.

"Yes. But I will return after two weeks."

"Good luck bro," Himanshu and I said.

"Thanks. Goodbye."

Three of us disconnected the call. Now, Sameer-Shalini controversy became the topic of discussion for many people. It gave a huge publicity to him. He became a national figure before anyone could see him on Splitsvilla. People started searching his comedy videos on YouTube. They got impressed by his desi jokes.

The top management of the media house in which Himanshu was interning was impressed by his spectacular work. They offered him a job at the news channel with an attractive package. I was also getting ready to depart for Bangalore.

I heard that Shalini couldn't file a case against Sameer because the case was transparent and all evidences were against her. Moreover, the case could infuriate Sameer's fans, who might stop using and prevent others to use the product of her father's company. So, she got underground.

After two weeks, Sameer returned to Mumbai. He first came to my room before going to his room.

"Hi Sam! How was the villa?"

"It was fantastic. There is some news. But promise me you won't tell anyone."

"I promise that I won't tell anyone."

"Actually I am the Splitsvilla winner of this season."

"Oh wow! Congrats! Cheers!"

"The organisers of the programme asked me not to disclose the information to anyone. But still I am telling you. Please don't tell anyone else."

"So where's the party?" I asked in excitement.

"Let's go to Juhu. We will find a nice restaurant out there. Call Himanshu too there."

"Do you know that Himanshu got a job offer in the same media house for a nice post?"

"Oh fantastic! So the controversy was a turning point for Himanshu and my life."

"Yes dude."

"Okay so I am leaving for my PG. We will meet at Juhu station at 8 pm."

Three of us met at the venue at 8 pm. We first walked along the Juhu beach and pulled each other's leg. Then we went to a nice restaurant in Juhu. We first ordered starters and then the main course. Suddenly a large mob appeared near our table. It consisted of the customers who came to the restaurant for dining.

"Hey! Aren't you the Desi Dude?"

"Yes," Sameer said shyly.

"We saw your videos on the YouTube," a young boy said.

"I saw you in an advertisement," a girl said in Marathi.

"Your body is dashing," a girl said.

"Thank you," Sameer said.

Sameer was blushing. Himanshu and I were just staring at him. The people started clicking selfies with him. People were jumping on each other to get a snap with him. The waiters rushed at the mob to control them. Three of us ate just the starters and left the restaurant.

"Hey Sameer, your fame will kill us," I said jokingly.

The Splitsvilla started broadcasting on MTV. People finally saw the local superstar on national television. The Shalini Verma controversy, along with his toned body, attractive look and sense of humour made him a huge celebrity. Even I was enjoying watching him on MTV.

"Cheers!"

Himanshu, Sameer and I organised a small party in Sameer's flat. We brought cold drink, tandoori chicken for snacks and tandoori roti and butter chicken for the dinner.

"Cheers for Sam's victory at the Splitsvilla. Long live his success," Himanshu cried, tearing the leg piece of the tandoori chicken.

"It's all because of you two bros. You helped me to expose Shalini and come out of her trap," Sameer said.

"We want to see you in a movie acting against Alia Bhat."

Sameer blushed after hearing her name.

"Let's see. But I got an offer to work in a Hindi daily

soap as the protagonist. Maybe I will get a chance to act in a mainstream movie shortly."

"You will, you will, you will... Kudos," I said.

We enjoyed a lot that night. We also held a small DJ night at his room by playing all the bollywood mashups. We ate the sumptuous dinner and ended our party with ice-cream. Three of us slept in his room and departed for our PGs the next day morning.

NINETEEN

Now it was my time to part with Sameer. It was September and I had to go to Bangalore to join the company. Sameer came to my PG in his new Maruti Suzuki Vitara Brezza to drop me at the Mumbai CST railway station. He was proud of his new car. I kept my luggage in his car and sat in the front seat. Sameer was wearing a hat and black goggles to hide his face.

We departed from Powai for the railway station. We started chatting while travelling.

"So finally, the day arrived, Sam." I said in a low voice.

"Yes Harry."

"Sam, when did you buy this car?"

"I bought it last week from the showroom near my rented flat. How is it?"

"It's fantastic, Desi Dude."

"I've been saving money since a long time to buy my own car."

"Wow. So what's your next agenda?"

"A big house in Mumbai."

I felt glad after hearing his dream. He drove through the busy streets of Mumbai and we reached the railway station after an hour. Sameer carried one of my bags to the railway station and I carried the remaining ones to the platform.

As we reached the platform, we kept our bags at a vacant place. The train didn't arrive at that time. Sameer turned to me to say something.

"Harry, as we are parting, I wish to confess something."

I thought he was going to admit any of his secrets to me.

"Yes sure, Sam."

"Actually that day, when you were talking to your mom, your conversation with your mom at a high volume woke me up. I got out of the bed and went near the terrace. I heard your conversation in which your mom was asking you to stay away from me…"

I was shocked to know that Sameer was aware of the whole incident.

"As you disconnected the call, I immediately lay down on the bed and closed my eyes to pretend that I didn't know anything. Next day I left early in the morning from the PG to find a rented flat for myself. I didn't want you to undergo the inconvenience of shifting with your project works and assignments. I could have stayed with you in the PG, but I didn't want to tarnish your relationship with your mom."

I stood in front of him with a head sunken down. But he held my palm.

"But I am not disappointed by this bro. Your mom was right. Both of us were able to focus more on our careers after parting with each other. If we stayed together, I would have ruined your career. But see now where we are- you got a nice placement and I got popularity."

A streak of happiness went through my face. The train arrived as we were talking. I boarded the train and asked him to sit with me in the compartment till the train leaves the platform. So he also boarded the compartment.

"Do you remember that both of us started our journey together in Rajdhani express five years ago?"

"Yes, I do remember."

"I will miss you dude."

"Whenever you miss me, just whatsapp me. I will call you back whenever I will be free."

The departure time of the train arrived. Both of us hugged each other and Sameer stepped down from the train. The train left the platform and I was waving at him and shouted, "Good luck bro."

"Good luck to you too," Sameer shouted.

The train left the station and gradually it disappeared. I went back to my seat. I sat down and thought about the journey of a guy from Sameer Mishra to the Desi Dude, his struggles and success. I was glad that I had been the eye witness of his journey. Though I knew that when even best friends enter into new lives, they slowly get disconnected, I didn't want to get disconnected from him. The sun had set and as the train was gaining momentum, the surroundings became darker.

I reached Bangalore next day afternoon. A cab was sent by the company to escort me from the station to the guest house. As I was sitting in the cab, the HR manager of the company called me. He asked me to join the firm from the next day. I reached the guest house in around half an hour. The guest house had lavish facilities. The company provided me the room as a part of my perk. The company arranged a lunch for me in the guest house. I spent the entire day filing my credentials to be presented in the company. I called Sameer in the evening.

"Hi Sam, I have reached Bangalore."

"Nice Harry. I have got an offer from the Rajshree Production for acting in their upcoming movie. I have accepted that offer and it will be my debut movie. The producers liked my performance in the Splitsvilla."

"Oh nice. What type of role is it?"

"It is a comedy role in which I have to play the character of a desi guy who cracks jokes and pulls the protagonist's leg."

"Wonderful!"

"My dream is to one day become the protagonist of a movie."

"You will definitely become one day."

" Now I have to leave for the gym. I will talk to you later. Bye."

"Okay bye dude."

Next day I went to my workplace. The head of the legal department introduced me to my other seniors and subordinates. He made me familiar with the working environment of the company. He also told me about the tasks that I needed to perform and my authority and responsibilities.

The days of my life at Bangalore slowly became mundane. I used to leave for the company at 8 am. The company provided me pick and drop facility. Then I worked till 6 pm, returned to the guest house and made power point presentations for the weekly departmental meetings. I asked a nearby dhaba owner to send north Indian food to my room against payment. In between, I used to call Sameer and Himanshu. The latter used to be free only after 10 pm and he picked my call only at that time. But I could rarely talk to the former. He used to be engaged in different tasks like stand-up comedy, film shootings, commercials, etc. throughout the day. After two months, Sameer's secretary used to pick up my call and he used to tell me a particular day and the timings in which I could call him.

I saw the full season of Splitsvilla. I saw those episodes more than once in which the scandal took place and that one in which he was called back to the programme. I enjoyed the grand finale in which he completed the given task efficiently with his new partner and won the season. I also saw his debut movie under the banner of Rajshree Production. He got the Filmfare Award in the same year for the best debut actor as well as the best actor in a comic role.

I met a woman named Madhuri Tripathi in Bangalore. She was from Allahabad. She worked in the logistics department of a travel agency. Both of us started meeting each other frequently in the Cafe Coffee Day and McDonalds. Slowly, we started liking each other, which changed in love. I proposed her six years ago, which she accepted. Both of us informed our parents about our relationship. Our families met in Bangalore and they liked each other. They instantly gave consent to the relationship. Madhuri and I were shocked to know that our fathers were old friends. So there was negligible chance of rejection of the proposal. My family whole-heartedly allowed her to continue her job after marriage.

We had a lavish wedding ceremony in Bangalore. We invited our relatives and friends to the ceremony. I sent wedding cards to Himanshu and Sameer too. Himanshu attended the ceremony, but Sameer couldn't come. I wished for his presence at the ceremony. However I received his gift a day after the ceremony, with a message of apology for not attending the wedding.

Madhuri and I saved money and bought a 3 BHK flat in Bangalore. The bank gave us loan. My parents stayed with us in the flat. Madhuri gave birth to our son a year after our marriage. It was the happiest moment of my life when I saw my son for the first time. My mother named him Sagar Shukla. Madhuri and my in-laws liked the name.

The birth of Sagar increased the work load of Madhuri. She faced problems in coping up with her deadlines and Sagar's tantrums. Her sweet smile and hearty laughter seemed to have eroded from her face. I got promoted to the post of Deputy Legal Advisor of my company and my work load increased.

Himanshu had an arranged marriage with a girl named Sakshi, who belonged to his native place. The marriage took place in Lucknow. He invited my family to the ceremony, but I couldn't attend it due to work pressure. He stays in a rented apartment in Mumbai with his wife. He had a daughter a month after the birth of Sagar. They named her Shivangi. They also purchased a small flat in Mumbai a year after the birth of their daughter.

I didn't want to get disconnected from Sameer, but his busy schedule and my work and family pressure separated us. I didn't get time to call him, nor did he. He rarely checked his whatsapp messages. I saw him only in Bollywood movies and commercials of exotic products like perfume, men's wear, breakfast cereals, etc. His personality was a perfect blend of sense of humour and an attractive body. Though I couldn't get connected to Sameer again, I hoped that he will prosper more in his career.

Epilogue

My nostalgia was shattered by the honking of the cars around my taxi. As my mind returned to reality, I saw that the taxi was standing at a traffic signal and it had turned green. It again started moving through a clear road.

"Memsahib, I told you that the traffic is temporary. Now the entire route will be free from any traffic congestions."

I saw Madhuri watching Desi Dude vines to deviate her mind from her stiff deadlines. She didn't pay attention to the driver's statement. Sagar was watching a cartoon on my i-pad and was giggling. I was happy that my wife and son were happy.

My mind again started pondering. Once I got a call from an unsaved number. I picked it up.

"Hello, Shukla," the voice said.

I instantly identified that it was Sameer.

"Oh Sam, how are you? After such a long time you have called."

"I am fine. I apologise for not being able to come to your wedding."

"Oh it's fine."

"What about your family, Shukla?"

"Madhuri is fine. She gave birth to our son four years ago. We named him Sagar."

"Oh wonderful. I was missing you and Himanshu a lot. So I am arranging a reunion of three of us with family. My secretary will whatsapp you my location. Tell me a date which will be suitable for you and bhabhi ji."

I thought for a while.

"We will be able to come to Mumbai after twentieth May. At that time, Madhuri's deadlines will be over and Sagar's nursery school will get closed in lieu of summer vacations."

"Nice. Himanshu will also be free at that time. So let's keep the date on May 25 at my residence. I will inform the date to Himanshu too."

"Okay dude."

"Desi Dude," he said jokingly.

"Yeah, Desi Dude."

"So, meeting you and your family on May 25."

He disconnected the call.

I again came back to reality. Madhuri agreed to accompany me to Mumbai as she never went to that city and she wanted to visit it. I didn't tell Madhuri that I was going to meet the Desi Dude, whose vines and movies are her favourite. I told her that one of my cousins, who stays in Mumbai, invited us. I was excited to see her reaction after she finds that the person is the Desi Dude.

The taxi reached his bungalow in Juhu. I was seeing his bungalow for the first time. It was a huge white coloured bungalow. It had large windows made up of glass. As Madhuri, Sagar and I stepped down from the taxi and went towards the gate, the watchman stopped us.

"Sir, can you tell me your name?"

"I am Harish Shukla."

"Let me talk to my master. Please wait for a while."

He dialled a number on the telephone and picked up the receiver.

"Sir, a man named Harish Shukla has come along with his family. Shall I allow them to enter the house?" the watchman said.

The voice inside the telephone told him to allow us to enter.

"Sir, you may enter. Welcome sir."

Three of us walked on a path, which had lush green lawn on both sides. We spotted a spectacular Range Rover car parked in front of the bungalow.

"You never told me that your cousin is so wealthy," Madhuri whispered in my ears.

I still didn't tell her the reality.

A young girl was standing near the bungalow. She came to us.

"Good afternoon Harish sir, ma'am and Sagar. Please come this way."

She ushered us into the bungalow and we went through a broad corridor. We came across few secretaries who were busy with computers and headphones. They were attending calls and setting appointments.

"Sir, he is busy on June 15. He is free on June 17. You

may shift the farewell party on that day, if you want his performance...," a secretary spoke.

"...ma'am, he has to perform at Narsee Monjee on July 15. Please select another date. Secondly, we will charge a fixed amount, Rs. 25 lakhs, non- negotiable," another secretary spoke.

"...Rakesh ji, sir will meet you on June 25 for your upcoming film in Studio number 10. Thank you Rakesh ji," another secretary said.

"...Sorry sir, he cannot perform at Maitryi College in the college Fresher's party as it is clashing with the Fresher's party of Janki Devi Memorial College, where we have already committed. We will surely contact you soon," another secretary said.

In the same way, we heard the words of other secretaries. They were setting and cancelling appointments. Madhuri turned to me and looked at me with suspicious eyes.

"Is your cousin a celebrity? Please be honest."

"Darling, you will come to know about my 'cousin' in a few minutes. It's a surprise."

"I can't wait any more, dear."

"Have patience. Just a few minutes, Madhuri."

Three of us came to the drawing room. Himanshu was sitting on the sofa with his wife and daughter. They stood up as they saw us.

"Hi Himanshu! We are meeting after such a long time."

Both of us hugged each other.

"Yes. How are you bro?"Himanshu said.

"Fine bro. This is my wife, Madhuri and son, Sagar."

"Namaste bhabhi ji. Hello Sagar," he said while moving his hand on Sagar's hair.

"Namaste bhaiya ji and didi," Madhuri said, controlling her eagerness to meet the 'cousin.'

"This is my wife, Sakshi and daughter, Shivangi."

"Namaste bhabhi ji. Hello princess Shivangi," I said.

Madhuri turned to me and spoke in my ears in a quick and hush voice, "Is he your cousin and his wife?"

"No no. He is my old friend Himanshu and his family. My 'cousin' will come in a few minutes."

"You have been telling this since ten minutes."

"What are both of you discussing in a hush voice?" Himanshu said with a wink.

"Actually I still haven't told Madhuri about the person whom we have come to meet. I have kept it suspense."

"Oh nice. I think that bhabhi ji will sprang up in amazement after seeing the guy," Himanshu said.

"You two old friends are increasing my curiosity. I can't control it further."

Both of us and Sakshi started giggling.

I ignored Madhuri's feelings and looked around the house. I saw large paintings on the walls and lavish furniture. I was surprised to find an earthen pot kept at a corner of a room. He used it in the PG and he has still preserved it. I saw a large portrait of Sameer's father with a large garland on it. It shows that he still loves and respects his father. I looked at the ceiling and saw a huge chandelier hanging from it. The floor had good quality marble.

The two ladies started talking among themselves. Suddenly an old lady in a white saree entered the drawing room. She was Sameer's mother. When she saw us, she had put a veil on her head. Madhuri and Sakshi also put a veil on their head.

"Namaste, aunty ji," four of us spoke in unison.

"Namaste, my dear children. Sam beta was eagerly waiting to meet you all. But he had to leave for an hour for an urgent meeting. He will return in a few minutes."

"Sam?" Madhuri said.

"My son..." Sameer's mother was about to speak out his name.

"Aunty ji, it's a secret," I chuckled.

"Sagar's dad, now you are being very mean," Madhuri said.

"Okay Harish beta. Shambhu, bring chilled soft drinks for our guests."

Shambhu, her attendant arrived with a tray with the glasses of soft drinks.

Suddenly, a loud voice came from the corridor.

"Hi guys, I am back. Sorry to keep you waiting. Now I am here."

All of us got excited.

Finally, Madhuri's wait was over. The Desi Dude entered the hall. Now he had a more muscular body and an attractive hair style. He wore a nice sweatshirt and Armani jeans.

"The Desi Dude! I can't believe that I am standing in front of him!" Madhuri exclaimed.

"Namaste Madhuri bhabhi and Sakshi bhabhi. Hello prince Sagar and princess Shivangi."

"Namaste Desi Dude," Sakshi, Sagar and Shivangi spoke

simultaneously. However, Madhuri was completely stunned and speechless.

"Madhuri, the Desi Dude was my roommate and my friend in the tuition classes. He is not my cousin, but a nice bro."

"Yes. Desi... I mean, bhaiya ji, I will take a photo with you. I want to make it my whatsapp DP."

"Yes sure bhabhi ji."

"Daughters, come with me. Let me show you the house. Let the sons sit together for their private talks."

The three ladies and the children left to see the entire house. Sameer, Himanshu and I sat on the sofa.

"So guys, how are your lives going on?" Sameer said.

"Nice Sam," Himanshu said.

"Nice. Now you are ruling the comedy world," I said.

"Not yet," Sam said.

"Sam, why haven't you married someone yet? You are in your thirties," I enquired.

"See guys, if I marry so early, how can I create new controversies each time and get attention of the media?"

"Shalini Verma controversy..." Himanshu chuckled.

We started laughing heartily.

"Well, I heard that recently you had a breakup with a model named Aisha Nathani. She was your fourth girlfriend, right," I said.

"Actually we didn't have anything between us. She was an aspiring model and I wanted to create some buzz for myself. We decided that we will create a fake love affair, so that both of us can get publicity."

"Oh you are very clever, Desi Dude," Himanshu said.

We again laughed.

"Then you will never be able to marry someone," I said.

"Oh doesn't matter," Sameer grinned.

"So your mom stays with you, dude," Himanshu enquired.

"Yes. Mom has grown old and weak, so she left her job at the day- care centre. Now, by God's grace, my income is enough to support our expenses..."

"Bro, your earning is in crores! It is more than enough, dude," Himanshu intervened.

Sameer grinned.

"We have let out the Delhi's house. We get a handsome rental income from it."

"Oh my God!" Himanshu said.

"So guys, what will you have, Blender's Pride, Black Dog or Bacardy? Don't be shy, your wives are not here," Sameer asked.

Himanshu and I turned to each other and then said, "Bacardy."

"Okay. Shambhu kaka, Shambhu kaka..." Sameer shouted. "Guys, he is cooking the lunch, so he couldn't hear us. Let me bring it myself."

Sameer left. Suddenly, Himanshu's mobile phone started ringing.

"Shukla, this is my boss's call. I have to take it."

"Yes sure."

Himanshu also left the room. I was looking around me again. I started thinking about Sameer's father. He always pestered him for studies, so that he can earn more money and settle his father's debt. But now, he is earning manifold amount than any academician, engineer or doctor. His wealth showed that his income can settle around ten such debts of his father. I wish his father were alive to see his success and wealth.

I saw a Filmfare magazine kept under the tea-table. I picked it up and saw the Desi Dude's photo on the cover page. He was standing in a blue T-shirt and white dhoti in front of a tractor, with his muscular body and black goggles on his face. The cover page had the caption, 'the Desi comedian of the box office, the Desi Dude.'

I was sitting on the sofa with the magazine in my hand. I was smiling, smiling and smiling...

About the Author

Date of Birth: 7th September, 1998

Place of Birth: New Delhi

das_**shubham**@rocketmail.com

This is the first novel written by Shubham Das. He was born on September 7, 1998 in New Delhi in a Bengali family. He studied at The Air Force School, Subroto Park, New Delhi. Currently, he is pursuing B.A. (Hons.) Economics from Kirori Mal College, University of Delhi. He has a knack of composing poems and reading and writing short stories since a very young age. He participates in various co-curricular activities. Apart from creative writing, Shubham Das has keen interest in music, especially Indian Classical Music. Currently, he lives in Rohini, New Delhi.

SHUBHAM DAS

Did you like the book

Email your questions, experiences, and suggestions to the author at das_shubham@rocketmail.com

Your Experiences